THE
CORPSE'S
TALE

KATHERINE JOHN

ACCENT PRESS I

Published by Accent Press Ltd – 2006
ISBN 190517319
Copyright © Katherine John 2006

The Quick Reads project in Wales is a joint venture between
the Basic Skills Agency and the Welsh Books Council.
Titles are funded through the Basic Skills Agency as part of
the National Basic Skills Strategy for Wales on behalf of the
Welsh Assembly Government.

Printed and bound in the UK by
Clays Plc, St Ives

Cover Design by Emma Barnes

FOR

PROFESSOR NORMAN ROBBINS

Who wanted to know what had happened to
Trevor Joseph

CHAPTER ONE

'HERE'S TO ANNA HARRIS. The next Catherine Zeta Jones to head for Hollywood from Wales.' Bob Evans, the richest farmer in Llan, lifted his glass to an eye-catching blue-eyed blonde. Anna was sitting, surrounded by women at a corner table in the bar of the Angel Inn.

'Thank you, Mr Evans.' Anna lifted her glass in return and every customer in the bar did the same. 'But I have three years in Drama School before I can think of Hollywood.'

'You'll get there, love.' Rita James, the landlord's wife, bustled over and collected empty glasses from Anna's table. 'I was only saying the other day, Anna's too pretty and talented to live out her life in a small village like Llan.'

'You deserve your scholarship, Anna,' Judy Oliver, the vicar's wife, agreed. 'Although I don't know what I'm going to do for a leading lady in the dramatic society after September.'

'Slap more greasepaint on the older members,' her sister-in-law Angela George, a police officer's wife, quipped. 'That's a stunning watch, Anna. It's like yours isn't it, Judy?'

'Similar,' Judy agreed.

'Isn't it gorgeous?' Anna held out her hand so they could admire the gold and diamond bracelet watch.

'Birthday present?' Angela asked.

Anna winked. 'From a secret admirer.'

'Say no more. I don't like romantic stories – they make me realize what I'm missing.' Rita carried the glasses into the kitchen where her plump, middle-aged husband, Tyrone, was refilling the ice bucket.

'Bob Evans is a dirty old man.' Rita dumped the tray on the draining board. 'He watches every move Anna Harris makes.'

'As does every man around here, love.' Tyrone shook more cubes into the bucket. 'There's no harm in looking. Anna's pretty enough to set any man's hormones raging, even one on the brink of the grave.'

'Which Bob Evans soon will be, if he carries on drinking at the rate he is.'

'Be glad he decided to spend his retirement here. Half our weekly profits are down to him.'

'Anna Harris is young enough to be his granddaughter.'

'And she'll be gone from here for good in a

couple of weeks, more's the pity.' Tyrone returned to the bar.

Anna finished her drink and draped her shawl around her shoulders.

'You're not going? I was just about to get in another round,' Angela complained.

'My parents are away at an antiques fair. I promised I'd open the shop in the morning.'

'Let's hope the fine weather brings out the tourists. The church fund could do with a boost.' Judy set up a stall every Saturday outside the church gate and sold honey and donated local produce to raise money.

'So could the shop. The more money Dad makes, the more generous he'll be to his poor student daughter. Goodnight everyone.'

Before Anna closed the door she heard Bob Evans say, 'Nice girl, that one. Got a kind word for everyone.'

She shuddered. She'd never liked Bob Evans. Even as a little girl she'd felt he was mentally undressing her.

She walked through the car park. The night air was warm, still and scented with roses and lavender. Lights shone in the rows of cottages and shops that bordered the road, but the village square was deserted. The medieval market place was shrouded in darkness beneath its slate roof. She loved Llan, its picture-postcard prettiness and friendly neighbourliness. She'd been fortunate to have been born and brought up in the place but it was time to move on. July was almost over; another month and she'd be living a new life in a city. If she was successful, she'd never spend another summer here.

Laughter from the Angel echoed behind her when she crossed the road. She rubbed a smudge from the corner of the glass in front of the church notice board and saw her mirrored reflection. Her long blonde hair shimmered silver in the moonlight and her pastel calf-length frock floated lightly around her slim figure. She pictured herself on stage – Titania in *A Midsummer Night's Dream* – or even better, Juliet.

She looked up and down one last time. Seeing no one, she opened the gate and ran up the path that led between the tombstones to the church. It was a shortcut the whole village used. The church was situated between the pub and shops on one side and rows of cottages on the other. It was easier to walk across the churchyard than around it.

Lost in thoughts of her glittering future, she passed the small shed behind the vestry at the back of the church. A hand shot out and clamped over her mouth. Helpless, unable even to scream, she was yanked into darkness, beneath a yew tree, too deep for moonlight to reach. The man whispered her name into her ear and lifted a finger to his lips before releasing her.

She locked her arms around his neck and kissed him passionately. He swung her off her feet and carried her to a raised tomb built against the church wall. Their figures merged and slipped low into the darkness.

Snatches of conversation continued to drift into the village square from the inn. The clock in the church tower struck ten and a dozen women tumbled out of the pub. They lingered, laughing and joking for a few minutes before heading off in different directions.

A man, thickset, heavily built, left the row of cottages on the opposite side of the church to the inn, opened the gate and shambled into the churchyard. Stooping low, he clicked his fingers and rattled a lead. He called out to every rustle in the shrubs planted among the graves. When he reached the gate that faced the Angel, he turned and retraced his steps.

He sobbed and wiped his eyes as he closed the gate behind him. He headed down the lane, past the cottages, still rattling the lead and calling out to every shadow that moved in the puddles of moonlight.

Tyrone ushered the last customers from the Angel and locked the doors. Men and women shouted "goodnight" before dispersing. Half a dozen women linked arms and danced into the market singing "I Whistle a Happy Tune".

One by one, the lights in the cottages and pub were extinguished. Cats prowled the street and gardens. A fox trotted across the churchyard, stopped and sniffed, only to run off at speed when a dog barked.

The figures in the shadows at the back of the church rose. They separated and merged again briefly before separating one final time. The man walked away quickly, towards the back of the churchyard. He vaulted the wall. Soon, he was lost to sight in a copse of trees.

Anna sat on the tomb and began to fasten the row of buttons on the bodice of her dress. An owl screeched and swooped low over a scuttling in the hedgerow of a cottage garden. She froze.

The gate at the cottages side of the yard creaked and Anna shrank against the wall. Footsteps crunched over the gravel path. They passed the church but she didn't move until she heard the gate close opposite the inn. Jumping down from the tomb she moved her feet over the grass, searching for her shoes. She found one, picked it up and slipped it on, lifting her leg to hook the back over her heel.

She sensed movement, glanced up, and saw the glint of reflected moonlight above her head. Before she had time to register what it was, it crashed down. She fell, swallowed by agonizing, unbearable pain. Lights swirled before her eyes. Unable even to crawl, she reached out, grabbed flesh and dug in her nails.

Her fingers weakened. The pools of moonlight merged with the shadows into unrelieved blackness. As the colour bled from the scene, so did her pain.

Badgers prowled, knocking over bins in search of food. The owl returned to its roost in a barn. Foxes rooted in the mess the badgers had left. But all was quiet when the first rays of the sun touched the eastern hills. It rose steadily and when the church clock struck five the valley was bathed in soft, golden light.

Tom the baker was the first to leave home. Dressed in his white overall, his chef's cap pushed to the back of his head, he closed his front door at five minutes past five and walked to his shop two doors up from the pub. Ten minutes later his apprentice hurtled down the road and banged on the shop door.

At six o'clock a van dropped off a bundle of newspapers outside the general store and Post Office. Three boys from the council houses arrived just as Gareth Morris, Postmaster, newsagent and store manager opened the door.

At half past six, the boys were out on the road with their newspaper-filled sacks. The church clock struck seven, the postman appeared and David "Dai Helpful" Morgan left his cottage in Church Row. He blew a kiss to his mother and crossed to the churchyard, his puppy, Sammy running at his heels.

Dai felt good. His mam had cooked him his favourite breakfast of bacon, eggs and leek and pork sausages. He'd chopped only half the load of logs Mr Jones had donated to the church and chopping was his favourite job. And his mam was roasting a chicken for dinner.

"Dai Helpful", as he was known to everyone in Llan, was thirty years old. He knew he was different from other men. His mother had explained that his brain had been starved of oxygen when he was born. That made him slower than most and not as clever. But his mam had taught him to be grateful for his good home and kind friends and neighbours.

The vicar, Mr Tony, employed him three days a week. Dai enjoyed keeping the church clean and the graveyard tidy. In summer he was offered more odd gardening jobs than he could do. In winter he walked people's dogs along with his own. And there was always someone who needed wood chopped, or trees trimmed. Mr and Mrs Harris, who lived next door to him and his mam, paid him to work in their antique shop on auction days to help with the lifting. Most weeks, he earned more than enough to pay his mam for his keep and buy his clothes and the odd pint of beer.

He headed for the shed where he kept his tools, then remembered he hadn't put his axe away the day before. He'd left it in the chopping block behind the shed. He hoped a child hadn't found it and hurt themselves.

Something glittered on the path and he picked it up. It was an earring, a gold one. There was dirt on it and he tried to rub it clean but the mark wouldn't come off. Sammy bounded ahead. He dropped the earring into his pocket and ordered Sammy back sharply. He was cross with Sammy for running off the night before. His Mam had told him to have more patience because the dog was young. But his last dog, Toby, had never run off, not even when he'd been a puppy.

Sammy slunk back with his tail between his legs. Dai crouched to pat him and saw a girl's legs behind the shed. He leaned forward. She was lying on the grass next to a tomb. An axe – his axe, he recognised the marks on the handle – in her head. He was so frightened he couldn't breathe.

He knew he should try to help her. The axe must be hurting her, so he lifted it. It came out easily. Too easily. He fell back on the path and cried out. His hands and shirt were covered with blood. And the girl still hadn't moved.

He looked up and saw Mr Tony staring at him.

'Someone put my axe in her head, Mr Tony. I took it out.'

The vicar's eyes rounded in horror.

'It wasn't me that put my axe in her head, Mr Tony. She'll tell you.' Dai looked back at the girl. Her head was covered in blood. She was naked. His mam had told him it wasn't right to look at naked girls. He turned away. But he could still see her foot. A fly landed on her toe. She still didn't move and she was stiff. As stiff as the animals the people in the village sometimes asked him to bury.

'It wasn't me that did it, Mr Tony,' he whispered. 'It wasn't me.'

CHAPTER TWO

TEN YEARS IN PRISON had changed Dai Helpful. He had learned not to get noticed. He never spoke unless someone spoke to him first. He stepped out of everyone's way. He never hit anyone back, no matter how hard they hit him. He also learned to look as though he was listening when he wasn't. He did that because of the bad language. His mam hated bad language. She told him so when she visited him. And reminded him in her weekly letters.

The judge finished speaking and the courtroom fell silent. Dai shuffled nervously in the dock. He didn't like courtrooms. There were no windows. The air was hot and stale. And people in courtrooms used big words he didn't understand.

Mr Smith was smiling at him, but Mr Smith had smiled at him the last time he'd been in a courtroom. Then he'd been made to sit for weeks and weeks, listening to people tell lies about him and Anna Harris. He hadn't been allowed to say what had really happened that morning in the churchyard. Afterwards, he had been sent to prison. And there he had stayed until now.

The judge leaned forward on the bench. 'Mr Morgan?'

Dai jumped at being spoken to directly, but he knew what to say. 'Yes, sir.'

'Do you understand what I've just said?'

Dai was afraid the judge would be angry with him for not paying attention, but he shook his head.

The judge turned to Mr Smith. 'Please explain the proceedings to your client.'

Alan Smith touched Dai's arm. He was still smiling. But Dai was too upset to smile back. Alan Smith was his "counsel". Dai didn't know what "counsel" meant but he knew Mr Smith was his friend. He had visited him in prison, especially at Christmas when it had been difficult for his mam to travel because the trains didn't run.

Mr Smith had brought him comics, Air Fix kits and sweets. More important he had listened to him. And Dai felt that Mr Smith believed him when he said he hadn't murdered Anna Harris. Anna had been kind to him. She had been his friend

'David.' Alan Smith's smile grew wider. 'You've won.'

Dai slipped his arms further up the sleeves of the jacket of the suit Alan had given him for court. It was the same one he had worn ten years before and he had lost weight in prison. 'Won what, Mr Smith?'

The judge said, 'You're free to go, Mr Morgan.'

Dai heard the judge but he didn't believe him.

'You're free, Mr Morgan,' the judge repeated.

Alan helped him from the dock. 'We'll telephone your mam to tell her you're coming home, David, and then I'll buy you a cup of coffee and a cake.'

Dai looked from Alan back to the judge. 'I don't understand.'

'You're free, David,' Alan repeated. 'You don't have to go back to prison.'

'My kits – my drawings – '

'We'll send someone to get your things, David.'

Dai couldn't believe it. 'I don't have to go back to prison?'

'No. The judge has looked at the evidence and declared your conviction unsafe.' Alan said slowly.

'I won't ever say I killed Anna Harris because I didn't.' Dai clamped his lips shut.

14

Alan remembered the parole board meetings. David had been offered early release from his life sentence on condition he admitted his crime and showed remorse. But David had the mind of a ten-year-old boy trapped in the body of a six-and-a-half-foot, two-hundred-and-fifty-pound body builder. There were a lot of things that he didn't understand. But he knew right from wrong because his mam had taught him. David knew it was right to tell the truth and it was wrong to tell lies. He wouldn't say sorry for killing Anna Harris because he hadn't killed her.

'You don't have to say that you killed Anna Harris, David,' Alan said. 'The judge has set you free because your conviction is unsafe.'

Dai didn't understand "conviction is unsafe". 'He knows I didn't kill Anna Harris, Mr Smith?'

'The judge says there's a possibility that you didn't.'

Dai's voice rose angrily. 'But I didn't kill her, Mr Smith, you know that.'

'I know, David. I have always believed you. Come on, it's time for you to go home.'

'Home to Mam?'

'Yes, David, home to your mam,' Alan echoed.

15

'Will everyone in the village know that I didn't kill Anna Harris now, Mr Smith? My mam knows, but there's Sergeant George, the Reverend and Mrs Tony, and Mr and Mrs James from the Angel, and Anna's mam...'

'I don't know about the people in the village, David,' Alan replied honestly. 'But the case will be reopened. The police will look at the evidence again.'

'Sergeant George...'

'Retired years ago, David, but the police from Llan won't be looking at the case. They'll bring in new police officers from another force.'

'And they'll know I didn't kill Anna, Mr Smith?'

'They'll study the evidence, David.' Alan nodded to the court officers clearing the courtroom. 'Let's telephone your Mam and get you home.'

Home. Dai pictured the village. His Mam's cottage in Church Row. He crossed off the days on his calendar every morning so he knew it was July. He had seen blue sky and green leaves on the trees through the small window in the van that had brought him to court. The roses and lavender would be blooming in his mam's garden. His mam would open the kitchen door and hug him. There'd be a fire in the range and the smell of roasting chicken, and apple and sage stuffing, roast potatoes and gravy.

'Home, David.' Alan pressed the search button on his mobile phone, and found David's mother's telephone number.

The call came through to Superintendent Bill Mulcahy's office at six o'clock. He had received a tip-off days ago that the "Churchyard Murder" would be referred to his division if David Morgan won his appeal. He spoke to HQ for twenty minutes, put down the receiver and walked into the office next door.

Newly promoted Inspector Trevor Joseph was sitting behind his desk shovelling files from his in-tray into his out-tray.

'Finished wrapping up the Jubilee Street murder, Joseph?'

'Last of the paperwork, sir.' Trevor eyed the Superintendent warily. His boss had already congratulated him on the job and he wasn't given to repeating praise.

Mulcahy sat in the visitor's chair. 'You been following the David Morgan case?'

'The Welsh churchyard murder?'

'That's the one. Do you have any thoughts on it?'

'I don't know anything other than what I've read in the papers.' Trevor's sense of unease grew. His honeymoon had been short and he'd been planning to take his wife on a break.

'What's that?' Mulcahy asked.

'Like every other story in the press it depends on the rag you're reading. You can take your pick as to whether David Morgan is a dangerous sub-human monster or a sad, brain-damaged man with the mind of a child.'

'How would you like to find out the truth?'

Trevor dropped the last file into his out-tray. 'I have put in for a week's leave, sir.'

'Postpone it until after you've re-opened and investigated the Morgan case and I'll make it two.'

'And if something else comes up in the meantime?' Trevor knew how worthless Mulcahy's promises were.

'I'll dump whatever it is on someone else.'

'Really, sir?'

Mulcahy chose to ignore Trevor's sarcasm. 'I'll ask them to send you the paperwork, then.'

Trevor knew from experience there was no point in fighting the inevitable. 'I'll need a team.'

'Who do you want?'

'Peter Collins.'

'He's a sergeant in the Drug Squad, not Serious Crimes.'

'He's a good copper.'

Collins had the reputation of being the most difficult officer in the force to work with. For some reason that Mulcahy had never worked out, Trevor Joseph got on with the man. 'Have him.'

'Sarah Merchant.'

'No chance, she's the best research assistant and computer expert we have.'

'Which is why I want her. You know what it's like to go through cold files.'

Mulcahy thought for a moment. 'Wrap the case up as quickly as you can. I want her back here in two weeks.'

'That might be pushing it, sir.'

'You're going to Mid Wales, you'll have nothing to do but work. Patrick O'Kelly has the post-mortem files on the victim. Pass my apologies on to your wife.' Bill went to the door.

'Do you have any thoughts on the Morgan case, sir?' Trevor asked.

'Thoughts,' Mulcahy repeated. 'I have plenty, Joseph. As for the truth – it's anyone's guess and for you to find out. Good luck.'

Patrick O'Kelly was drinking coffee from a specimen jar in his office in the mortuary when Trevor called the next morning. Aware of Patrick's workload, Trevor had made an appointment. Patrick had the file open and the photographs ready.

'Professor Norman Robbins did the original post-mortem, retired now. Thorough guy, he did a brilliant job but you lot slipped up.'

'We did?' Knowing better than to expect a "good morning" from Patrick, Trevor sat in the visitor's chair.

'Your lot sent less than half the samples Robbins took for analysis. But they've survived. We found them in the freezer.' Patrick laid a photograph of Anna Harris lying on a mortuary slab, on the desk. Her face was grey in death but still beautiful – and unmarked. Her skull, split across the crown of her head, gaped open, revealing grey-green brains. 'Death was caused by a single massive blow to the head.'

'Instantaneous?'

'No, but within minutes, in Robbins' estimation based on blood loss, less than five. He took dozens of swabs. There was evidence she'd had sex shortly before death but there was no bruising or injury to suggest she was forced. Robbins made a list of significant

20

findings.' O'Kelly referred to his notes. 'A stray pubic hair, black – not blonde like Anna's – was stuck on her upper thigh with semen. He bagged it and the semen, but it was never sent to the lab.'

'So we have DNA.'

'Of someone she almost certainly had sex with, but not necessarily her killer. There were scrapings of skin and blood beneath her fingernails...'

'You said there was no sign of force.'

'Not as in a typical rape. You expect bruising to the thighs, ribcage or the arms if the victim was held down. All you have here are skin scrapings.'

'Perhaps she saw her killer coming at her and lashed out?'

'It's for you to paint the picture, Joseph. All I can give you are the facts.'

It wasn't the first time Patrick's cold scientific approach had irritated Trevor. 'Was the skin tested for DNA and blood group?'

'Not tested at all. Did David Morgan have scratches on him when he was picked up?'

'I don't know.'

'If he did, it might explain why the police didn't bother.' O'Kelly set a photograph of Anna that had been taken in the churchyard

21

next to the one that had been taken in the mortuary. 'Spot the difference.'

'She was wearing a watch when she was found. It was removed for the post mortem. That's standard procedure.'

'It's an expensive gold and diamond bracelet watch in perfect condition. Look at her wrist after it was removed.'

Trevor picked up the photograph and peered at it.

'I had it blown up.' Patrick handed him a close up.

'Bullet wound?'

'Robbins said it was made by a narrow sharp pointed instrument, possibly a hiking pole with the safety end removed. And whoever did it used considerable force. There were splinters in the wound. Of what I don't know. They were bagged, but like so many other samples never sent for analysis. The injury was inflicted after death. Someone took off her watch, speared her wrist and then replaced the watch.'

'Could David Morgan have taken it as a trophy, kept it overnight and returned it in the morning?'

'You're the detective, Joseph.'

'The samples Robbins took…'

'Were sent to the lab last night. Don't expect

miracles after ten years.' Patrick lifted his specimen jar. 'Coffee? We may even have some chocolate biscuits in the fridge.'

CHAPTER THREE

'I'D FORGOTTEN WALES WAS so pretty. The countryside around here is lovely, it reminds me of Devon,' Trevor commented.

The sign for the end of the motorway flashed up and Peter Collins slowed the car. 'Very pretty,' he agreed dryly. 'Hills, fields, hedges, sheep, grass. Hills, fields, hedges, sheep grass – wait, I can see two cows and three trees.' He negotiated a roundabout and turned on to a narrow two-lane road. 'You sure about the B road number? That signpost didn't mention Llan.'

'But it did name the town before it, and the one after.' Trevor opened the file on his lap.

'Where are we staying again?' Peter slowed behind a tractor that was doing a steady ten miles an hour.

'The Angel Inn.'

Peter blasted his horn. 'If I read that signpost right, we're in the Bible belt of Britain.'

'It did say Sodom and Gomorrah, but the arrows were pointing in different directions.'

Trevor winced when Peter hit the horn a second time. 'Where do you expect that man to go?'

'Off the road and into a field.'

'I can't even see a gate.'

'He can go through a hedge can't he?'

Trevor pulled a sheet of paper from the file. 'I hate cold cases.'

'Mulcahy knows that, which is why he gave you this one. What I don't understand is why you had to drag me along.'

'Admit it, you're flattered.'

'To be ordered to follow you into the back of beyond?' Peter questioned. 'I most certainly am not. I feel as though I've been sent into exile.'

'It will be a nice break. Us working together just like the old days.'

'I like the new days. Having my own desk in our nice cosy station and my nice cosy life where I get to cuddle my girlfriend at night. At last.' The tractor turned off and Peter put his foot down, only to slam on the brakes again when a herd of cows blocked the road.

'Joys of country living.' Trevor hid a smile at Peter's annoyance.

'Joy nothing.' Peter pressed the button that wound up the electric window. 'It's bad enough seeing them without smelling them too.'

Trevor glanced at the file. 'Anna Harris was murdered ten years ago this week.'

As they were marooned in a sea of cows, Peter switched off the engine and waited for the animals to turn up the farm track to the milking sheds ahead. 'Seeing as how we're here until the cows go home, you may as well fill me in. Sorry I couldn't go to the briefing.'

'More like *wouldn't*,' Trevor corrected.

Peter gave Trevor a toothy smile. 'All perfect, but only as a result of two hours of agony at the dentist.'

'You don't have to give excuses to me. I'm not your teacher.' Trevor turned the page. 'Facts, David Morgan was arrested at the scene of the crime, charged with Anna's murder within twenty-four hours and the case against him prepared in a month by the local force. It took six months to come to court because David Morgan's defence team wanted medical and psychiatric reports. Due to an accident at birth he has a mental age of ten.'

The car rocked when a cow nudged it. Peter leaned back in his seat and closed his eyes. 'And we're expected to find out ten years later if the locals set up the village idiot as the fall guy?'

'According to the defence, David Morgan wasn't that much of an idiot. He held down a part-time job as caretaker of the local Church and kept the graveyard tidy. He also did odd jobs for people in the village, the landlord of the Angel Inn, the local doctor and several of the neighbours, including the victim, Anna Harris's parents.' Trevor pulled a photograph from the file. 'Pretty girl.'

Peter opened one eye and gazed at the studio portrait of a young woman with long blonde hair and bright blue eyes. 'Very,' he agreed. 'What do we know about her?' He closed his eyes again.

'Anna Harris, eighteen years old, had just taken her A levels and was guaranteed a place at Drama College. She had experience as a child actor and model, mainly catalogue work and as an extra in TV productions. She was spending her last summer at home with her parents, helping them out in their antique shop and auction house.'

'Boyfriend?'

'Several, nothing serious,' Trevor continued to turn the pages of the file. 'According to her mother she was determined to make a career as an actress and she avoided emotional entanglements.'

'So, she was ambitious. Friends?'

'The entire village, if the reports are to be believed.'

'Male or female?'

'Both.'

'Enemies?' Peter asked.

'None.'

'That I don't believe,' Peter said flatly. 'Isn't it considered unlucky for the Welsh to speak ill of the dead?'

'Not that I've heard. You into making up myths now, Collins?'

'Just something I heard somewhere,' Peter replied. 'What do we know about her movements the night she was killed?'

'She worked in her parents' antique shop from nine in the morning until six in the evening. Then she went home. From seven until nine o'clock she was at an amateur dramatics society rehearsal in the local community centre. The society was run by the vicar and his wife, Tony and Judy Oliver. They were preparing to put on a show in August. The last one Anna would star in before she left for college. It was *The King and I*, Anna, unsurprisingly, was to play Anna.'

'How many were at the rehearsal?'

'Sixteen gave witness statements. At nine o'clock twelve of them went to the Angel Inn.

28

Anna Harris went with them and drank half a pint of cider.'

Peter sat up and opened his eyes to see a cow staring at them through the windscreen. 'Tell me, as a farmer's son, can you say shoo to a cow?'

'You can say what you like, whether it will shoo or not is an entirely different matter,' Trevor answered.

Peter turned the ignition. As the engine purred into life the cow moved slowly away. 'Did Anna go home by herself that night?'

'Yes. She was the first to leave the pub at around ten o'clock. Her parents were away for the weekend on business and she was going to open their shop for them in the morning. She would have intended to cross the churchyard. It's a short cut from one side of the village to the other and used by everyone who lives there. It shouldn't have taken her more than five minutes to walk from the Angel Inn to her parents' cottage. The local boys don't believe she reached there. Her body, with David Morgan sitting next to it, was found shortly after seven o'clock the next morning in the churchyard by the vicar.'

'Do we have the post mortem report?'

'Yes and photographs. I've already gone

through both with Patrick O'Kelly. According to him the man who did the post mortem,' Trevor flicked through the file again, 'a Professor Robbins, was thorough, but more than half of the samples he took were never analysed.'

'But they are in the lab now?' Peter checked.

'Yes.'

'I hope they'll be enough. I hate exhumations even more than you hate cold cases. She was buried, not cremated?' he asked.

'In Llan Church,' Trevor confirmed. 'Let's hope we can leave her there in peace.'

'Results of the post-mortem report?'

'She was bludgeoned to death with an axe. Single blow. There's no doubt that it belonged to David Morgan. He normally kept it, along with other tools, in a shed at the back of the church but he said he forgot to put it away the night before the murder. He even identified the markings he'd made on the handle. His face, hands and clothes were stained with Anna's blood. His story was, he saw a girl he didn't recognize as Anna lying behind his tool shed when he turned up for work that morning. He thought she was still alive and tried to help her. Unfortunately for forensics, by pulling the axe from her head.'

'When was she killed?'

'According to the pathologist who tested her stomach contents – she ate peanuts in the pub as well as drinking cider – anything between one and three hours after she left the pub. That puts her death somewhere between eleven that night and two in the morning.'

'So if David Morgan *did* kill her it would be a case of the murderer returning to the scene of the crime several hours after the event.'

'It would.' Trevor referred back to the file. 'The police found one of Anna's earrings in David's pocket. It was bloodstained. He insisted he had picked it up on the path in the churchyard that morning a few minutes before he found Anna's body.'

Peter nodded. 'Give the man the benefit of the doubt and it's feasible. The murderer drops the earring, David Morgan picks it up. He stumbles across the body. There must have been more hard evidence than that against him.'

'Several witnesses saw him out looking for his dog from ten minutes past ten until midnight the night before, in the vicinity of the churchyard. That gives him time and opportunity.'

'Did anyone hear anything? Screams, cries?

'Nothing.'

'An axe isn't your usual murder weapon. Why did David have one at all?' Peter changed down a gear as they drove up a steep hill.

'The church uses a wood burning stove in winter. Farmers donated wood after land clearance, and David chopped it,' Trevor explained.

'And possibly pretty girls?' Peter looked sideways at Trevor. 'All right, we have timing, weapon, bloodstains and earring, what else?'

'Very little from what I can see,' Trevor thumbed through the papers.

'Motive? I take it she was sexually attacked.'

'Pathologist found evidence of sexual activity but not violent rape. She had been stripped naked, her dress was found nearby, as was one earring, but her underclothes were missing. David had the second earring but the underclothes were never found.'

'Forensic evidence?'

'Apart from the bloodstains on David Morgan's clothes, hands and face nothing that I can see here.'

'The axe?'

'No prints other than David's and no blood or DNA on it other than his and Anna's.'

'The earring?'

'Partial thumbprint and fingerprint, both David Morgan's. The blood was Anna's.'

'If that's it I'm not surprised Morgan was freed on appeal. The best you can say about the evidence is that it's circumstantial. The worst that it's a fit-up job. Is Morgan back in Llan?'

'Arrived two weeks ago.' Trevor saw the signpost for the village and closed the file.

'It will be interesting to see what kind of reception he received.' Peter stopped the car in a viewing lay-by and looked down on the scattering of houses clustered around a church and a road that cut through the valley.

'Very,' Trevor agreed.

'One thing is certain, Joseph. We should have this wrapped up in record time. There'll be nothing to do here except work.'

'And drink in the pub.'

Peter smiled. 'That too.' He pushed the car into gear and edged back out on the road.

CHAPTER FOUR

'I'M GLAD SOME PEOPLE like living in a place like this.' Peter drew up in the car park of the Angel Inn.

'Really?' Trevor studied the pub that would be "home" until they finished working on the Harris case. It looked ancient, long, low-built with small windows set in thick stone walls, it was painted a garish pink.

'They leave more room for the likes of us in the towns and cities, Joseph. Do you think there were ever enough people in this village to fill that church?' He pointed across the road. Llan Church was massive; built of granite on a low hillock on the floor of the valley, it dwarfed the surrounding buildings. It was also a carbon copy of a dozen others he'd seen since they had crossed the Severn Bridge into Wales.

'Possibly, from the number of gravestones around it.' Trevor stretched. It had been a long drive and the last forty miles on narrow, winding roads had felt like eighty. An appetizing smell wafted from an extractor fan set in the wall of the pub, reminding him he was hungry.

Peter glanced at his watch. 'Lunch time. Our dogsbody's van is here, so she will have set up shop.'

'Don't let me hear you calling her that again.' Trevor liked and respected Constable Sarah Merchant and suspected she would soon make sergeant. She had often tracked down leads and information when the officers in charge of a case had felt they'd come to a dead end. She was also immune to Peter's chauvinism and angry outbursts whenever he became irritated. Which was often.

'You're travelling heavy, Joseph.' Peter handed him a suitcase twice the size of his own.

'We don't know how long we'll be here.'

'Even a village like this must have a laundry.'

'I wouldn't bet on it.'

'Launderette?' Peter looked up the street. He saw a baker's, butcher's, chemist, antique shop, and what looked like a Post Office, general store and newsagent in one. He handed Trevor one of the large boxes of paperwork that hadn't been computerized, picked up his case and another box, and ducked under the low lintel into the pub.

The landlady, Rita James, had obviously been watching them from the window. She wiped her hands on her apron and stepped behind the small reception desk in the passageway. 'I don't need to ask who you are.' She opened the register and held out a pen.

Peter took it. 'Single room en suite?' he asked hopefully.

'We have no singles, only doubles. I warned the officer who made the booking I'd have to charge extra for all four. We only have the five rooms and with you taking four at the height of the season it's going to affect trade.'

Peter had a sudden vision of people flocking into Llan and demanding accommodation. The only problem was, he hadn't seen any other cars on the road for the last five miles.

'I'm Rita James, the landlady;, I look after the rooms and the restaurant and my husband, Tyrone, manages the bar and the cellar. You want anything you come to us. Although I'm not afraid to tell you I don't know why you're here and neither does anyone else in the village.'

'Why's that, Mrs James?' Trevor asked.

'Because we all know who killed poor Anna Harris, that's why. Dai Helpful should never have been freed. Its bad enough they don't hang people these days without letting people out of prison after they've served a couple of years. Life should mean life when you've taken one. Especially that of an innocent young girl. Anyway, that's what we all think around here.'

Trevor was taken aback by Rita's anger. 'We're here to find out the truth, Mrs James.'

'Sergeant George found that out ten years ago.' She snatched the pen from Peter and handed it to Trevor.

'If that's the case, we'll confirm his findings and be on our way in a couple of days,' Peter assured her.

The landlady frowned. 'You're not here to whitewash Dai Helpful and make Sergeant George look a fool?'

'As my colleague said, Mrs James, we're here to find out the truth.' Trevor signed his name below Peter's.

'Constable Merchant arrived an hour ago,' she said in a friendlier tone. 'She's in the room you booked as an office. Room one, first right at the top of the stairs. You're in three and four, Constable Merchant is in two.'

'Thank you, Mrs James. What time do you finish serving lunch?'

'Food is served all day, midday till ten at night. Last orders, half past nine. Breakfast is served in the back bar from half past seven to nine.'

'That is music to an overworked police officer's ears, Mrs James,' Peter gushed.

'We'll be down to look at the menu as soon as we've unpacked.' Trevor went to the stairs.

'It's on the blackboard in the bar. Nothing fancy, plain home cooking.'

'Sounds perfect to me.' Peter picked up his box and case.

'If you need help with those, I can call my Tyrone.'

'We can manage, Mrs James, thank you.' Peter ran up the stairs behind Trevor, his small suitcase balanced on top of a box of files.

'Will you look at this', Peter teased when he walked into the hotel room that was to be their "incident room" for the duration of their enquiries. 'The girl arrived only an hour ago and she's already unpacked her magic machine. Got the coffee sorted and bought chocolate biscuits as well, Sarah?'

Sarah ignored Peter and spoke to Trevor. 'I've given Patrick O'Kelly's office the landline number here and told them to telephone any test results directly to us, sir. I've also located the current addresses of Sergeant George who carried out the original investigation and Anna's mother. Her father killed himself the day after Anna's funeral. Her mother sold up and moved to Swansea shortly afterwards.' She held up two discs. 'Film taken at the murder scene and one of Anna's funeral. The DVD is connected to the TV.'

'Film of Anna's funeral?' Peter questioned.

'Taken by the local photographer. He made a fortune selling stills to the local and national papers.'

'Money grubbing...'

'He donated all the proceeds to Anna's memorial fund.' Sarah stopped Peter mid-flow.

'Good work, Constable,' Trevor said.

'I've run police checks on all the locals. Aside from minor parking and traffic offences, two farmers – Bob Evans and Harry Jones – were fined for not declaring income to the Inland Revenue. The landlord here, Tyrone James, was charged with affray but found not guilty in court. The vicar, Tony Oliver, was arrested ten years ago for possession of cannabis but never charged. His wife was charged with assaulting a woman Tony was having an affair with twelve years ago. It couldn't have been serious. She was bound over to keep the peace. No sex crimes or other serious assaults that I could find. And that is about all I've done so far, sir.'

'As the three of us are going to be living and working here until this case can be closed again, I suggest we drop the formality. Call me Trevor.'

'And me Peter.'

'I'd prefer to call you Sergeant Collins.' Sarah handed Peter a file. 'I've downloaded the trial transcripts and evidence files for you. As you missed the briefing I thought you should have your own copies.'

'Thank you, Constable Merchant.' Peter snatched them from her.

'Hungry?' Trevor asked.

'Yes – Trevor,' Sarah replied.

'Let's go and eat.'

'Given that everyone in the village probably thinks the same way as the landlady, we could eat up here and brainstorm at the same time,' Peter suggested.

Trevor shook his head. 'We'll eat in the pub, we'll socialise in the pub and we'll talk to the locals there. I doubt many besides Anna's mother have moved away in the last ten years. You never know what we might pick up.'

'Do you really expect to find new leads after ten years, sir?' Sarah asked.

'We won't know until we try. After we've eaten, Peter can help you sort this room before he catches up with his reading.'

'And where will you be?' Peter asked.

'Visiting David Morgan and his mother. The sooner we get his side of the story, the sooner we can begin our investigation.'

The bar fell silent when Trevor led the way in. He smiled at the room in general and read the blackboard. It didn't take him long to make a choice. 'Rump steak, chips, and a pint of Guinness.'

'Make that two,' Peter said, and 'Good afternoon,' to the silent, staring customers, before sitting at a table.

'Sarah?' Trevor asked.

'Tuna salad and a glass of mineral water please.' She sat opposite Peter.

'You'll get healthy, eating food like that,' Peter warned.

'Unlike you I care about my figure, Sergeant.'

'Ooh, you can be nasty, Merchant.'

'No winding anyone up on this case, Collins.' Trevor set the drinks on the table.

'Do you want us to put your food and drink on your bill, Inspector Joseph?' Tyrone shouted loud enough for all the customers to hear.

'Please, but itemise everything.' Trevor waited for someone to comment. He didn't have to wait long.

'You the police?' A weather-beaten middle-aged man sitting on a stool at the bar challenged.

'We are,' Trevor answered pleasantly. 'And you are?'

'Bob Evans, I farm up top. I hope the poor taxpayers, me included, aren't paying for your beer.'

'You're not. That's why I asked the landlord to itemise the bill,' Trevor explained.

'You're wasting your time and our money if you're here to reopen the Dai Helpful case.'

'Why's that?' Peter sipped his Guinness.

'Because Dai Helpful's as guilty as Cain, that's why. And what do you know about the case anyway?' Bob snapped. 'We don't need outsiders coming in here and telling us what's what. Sergeant George did a damned good job ten years ago. Not that he had that much to do,' he added. 'It was an open and shut case.'

'Officers from another force are always brought in when a case is reopened, it's government policy,' Trevor said mildly. 'Fresh eye and all that. And it's routine to reopen cases when an appeal against a conviction is successful.'

'No fresh eye needed here. Dai Helpful was found sitting next to the girl, covered with her blood. And it was his axe that was stuck in her head. How much more evidence do you need than that?' Bob demanded.

'The girl had been killed eight to ten hours before,' Peter reminded him.

'When Dai Helpful was out looking for his new puppy – or so he said,' Bob sneered. 'It's a case of the murderer returning to the scene of the crime. He raped and killed her and stripped her naked the night before and he couldn't stay away. He wanted to gloat over what he'd done. That's why he was there. According to every true crime book I've read, it's a textbook case.'

'It won't do any harm to take another look at the case, seeing as how the judge saw fit to set Dai Helpful free.' Tyrone was expert at diffusing arguments before they started. 'From what you told the missus you're not here to prove Dai innocent. If he's guilty you'll say he is.'

'If that's our conclusion,' Trevor agreed.

'And then they'll put him back where he belongs – in prison?' Bob demanded.

'It's not quite as simple as that,' Trevor said. 'He's already served ten years.'

'Not bloody long enough for a young girl's life.' Bob hit the bar, and the glasses hanging above it rattled. 'Life should mean life. Though why we have to keep the buggers in prison when we can save the expense and hang them is beyond me.'

'Few people in Llan will disagree with you there, Bob.' Tom the baker carried a pint of cider and a pork pie to a table.

'But it would be awful if that judge was right and Dai Helpful didn't kill Anna,' interjected a female voice.

Everyone turned towards the barmaid, a slight young girl with dark hair and eyes who looked too young to be working in a pub.

She lifted her chin defiantly. 'Well it would, wouldn't it?' she challenged.

'What would you know about it, Lily Jenkins?' Bob snarled. 'You were in nappies when Anna Harris was murdered.'

'I was ten years old, Mr Evans,' Lily corrected. 'And I only said it would be awful if Dai Helpful was innocent. It's not as if the police haven't made mistakes before. Three Cardiff men spent four years in prison for murdering a prostitute in Cardiff Docks only to be cleared later. And those two brothers from Swansea spent seven years in prison before being found innocent...'

'That's not the case with Dai Helpful,' Bob interrupted sternly.

'No doubt about it.' Rita set Sarah's tuna salad in front of her. 'Dai Helpful was born weak in the head and he did for her.'

'Bloody law,' Tom swore between bites of pork pie. 'Dai got off on a technicality and now they've let him out it'll be too late for the next poor girl he tops.'

'Just let him show his face near me, that's all I say,' Bob threatened.

'David Morgan is back in the village, isn't he?' Peter asked.

'Aye, but he hasn't had the gall to step out of doors because he knows what's waiting for him if he does,' Bob said darkly.

CHAPTER FIVE

RITA JAMES GAVE TREVOR directions to the Morgans' cottage. The quickest route was across the churchyard. Trevor knew he was following the exact same path Anna had taken the night she'd been killed.

He walked out of the car park on to the pavement. He crossed the quiet road, to the church notice board, depressed the latch on the roofed gate and closed it behind him. The churchyard was still, the air buzzing, alive with insects. It was hot even for July, just as it had been ten years before for Anna Harris. The reports he had read had been thorough. A full moon, clear sky, the temperature 26 degrees Centigrade, warm for a summer's day, let alone night.

He noted the dates on the tombstones. Like most churchyards still in use, there was a mix of ancient, old and new. The most recent were closest to the path. Low plain stones in black or white marble, with simple inscriptions and even simpler decorations. A cross or abstract pattern alongside or above the name. But he failed to find Anna Harris's grave. The more elaborate Victorian memorials were massive in comparison, some six feet high and more. A few were decorated with classical sculptures and Gothic lettering.

He had seen photographs of the churchyard taken on the day of Anna's murder. They had shown gleaming, scrubbed gravestones, neatly trimmed shrubs and bushes and cut grass. Now, the grass was higher in places than the ancient Celtic crosses and Victorian monuments and the shrubs were unkempt and covered in dead flower heads. The stalks of the spring bulbs had dried to straw. Weeds poked through the gravel on the paths and the older tombs were covered in moss.

The churchyard reminded him of so many other cemeteries he had seen in England and Wales. Forlorn, neglected, it was the reason he had added a clause to his will requesting that his body be cremated and his ashes scattered from the nearest cliff top to his parents' farm in Cornwall.

He spotted the shed he had seen in the scene of crime photographs. It, too, was dilapidated. The wood was rotting at the base of both the shed and the door and the roof felt was torn. If David Morgan had left any tools in it, they'd be useless. He tested the lock on the door. It was sealed solid with rust.

'Can I help you?'

Trevor eyed the man who had walked out of the back door of the church. The police habit of outlining a description was ingrained. Height, five feet ten inches, age, 40-ish, slim, athletic build, dark hair flecked with grey, styled to disguise the fact that it was thinning, grey eyes. He was wearing a dog collar on his lightweight grey summer shirt, grey slacks, black socks and slip-on loafers. He also looked familiar. Trevor was certain he had seen him before.

Trevor held out his hand. 'Inspector Trevor Joseph. I'm with the police team who are re-examining the David Morgan case.'

'Tony Oliver, vicar of St David's.' He shook Trevor's hand. 'Poor Anna Harris. That was a bad business.'

'Murders generally are.' Trevor looked at the shed. 'Is this where David Morgan kept his tools?'

'Yes, but the police took them when they arrested him.'

'They weren't returned?'

'To be truthful, Inspector Joseph, I didn't ask for them. I couldn't have brought myself to use them and I doubt anyone else in the village could have either.'

'Who has looked after the churchyard since David Morgan was arrested?'

'We set up a volunteer committee. It worked well for a few years but lately,' Tony shrugged his shoulders, 'no one's heart seems to be in it. My wife and I do what we can. It's not easy trying to run a parish and look after the fabric of the building and the graves.'

'It is a lot of work, given the size of the place,' Trevor agreed.

'Have you come to any conclusions yet?'

'Hardly, we only arrived in the village a couple of hours ago, Reverend Oliver.'

'I don't envy you, Inspector. Sergeant George investigated every possibility at the time. Everyone, including me, is absolutely sure he charged the right man.'

'You found Anna, didn't you?' Trevor knew the vicar had.

'Yes.'

'And David was standing over the body?'

'Crouched next to her.' Tony shook his head as though he wanted to be rid of the memory.

'Did David Morgan say anything to you?'

'I gave a full statement at the time, which will be more accurate than anything I can say now. Time has a habit of blurring conversations and events. But should there be anything that you think I, or my wife, can do to help you with your enquiries, please don't hesitate to call. You're staying at the pub?'

'Yes.'

'Rita has my telephone number. Parish business often keeps us from home. We live in the vicarage.' He indicated an imposing Georgian house that overlooked the churchyard.

'Very nice,' Trevor said.

'From the outside. The plumbing's a nightmare. It has twenty rooms, every one of them too large to heat to a comfortable level, which means we freeze in winter. But,' he made a wry face, 'as you said, it does look impressive.' He glanced at his watch. 'I hope you weren't coming to see me, Inspector. I'm due to administer communion in the local hospital in ten minutes.'

'I'm on my way to visit David Morgan.'

'I've just come from there.'

'How is he, Reverend Oliver?' Trevor asked.

'Call me Tony, everyone does, except David. He is as well as can be expected, considering what happened this morning.'

'There's been an incident?'

'Of course, if you've only been here a couple of hours you wouldn't have heard. Stones were thrown through his mother's window. There was a note on one of them.'

'What did it say?'

'Something unpleasant, Inspector. Sergeant Thomas was there when I left. If you're quick you might catch him.'

Trevor suddenly realized where he'd seen Tony Oliver before. 'You used to be Tony Jordan the singer. You had four number one hits.'

'Fifteen years ago in another more shallow life, Inspector,' Tony smiled. 'I will pray for you but I don't envy you your task. Much as I would like to think otherwise, given the years I've known him and his mother, Dai Helpful killed Anna Harris.'

'Because the alternative is too horrible to contemplate?' Trevor suggested.

'What is the alternative, Inspector?'

'That a murderer has been walking free among you for the last ten years while an innocent man has been locked up.'

Tony fell silent for a while. 'It's been nice to meet you, Inspector, but I must go. God speed.'

Tony walked off quickly. Trevor remained and studied his surroundings.

Llan church had been built on a low rise on the floor of the valley. The church itself blocked the view on one side. Trevor walked past the shed and stood in front of it. He had an uninterrupted view of the pub and row of shops on one side of the village and the cottages and their gardens on the other. Behind the shed was a large, high flat tomb, hidden from view by the church on one side, the shed on the other and an enormous yew tree on the third. He recalled what Patrick had said about Anna having sex before she died.

The spot certainly provided privacy for lovers who had nowhere else to go. And Anna had been found behind the shed, just two or three feet from the tomb. Had it been a meeting placed for her and one of her many "boyfriends"? But why risk meeting here that night? Her parents were away and their cottage was less than five minutes' walk. Were the neighbours watching her? Even if they were narrow-minded enough to monitor the movements of an eighteen-year-old girl about to leave home, Anna could have smuggled him through the back door.

Perhaps he was someone she dare not be seen with, especially late at night. Not a classmate or even a young man. But a married man. That's if he even existed. Trevor knew he was building a case on the flimsiest supposition. He could almost hear Collins and Mulcahy laughing at him.

He sat on the edge of the tomb to test his theory that he couldn't be seen from the village. The yew tree would have grown in ten years. He made a note to check how much. Even in daylight all he could see was a small triangle of churchyard between the tree and the shed.

He listened to the small noises of the village. A van with an old and, judging by the noise, tired diesel engine drove up the road. A tractor droned in a distant field. A child cried in one of the cottage gardens. Women's voices echoed from the covered market place, which according to the information in the pub, was only used on a Wednesday. Then he heard the tread of feet crunching over gravel.

He left his hiding place. Two women, their arms full of flowers, were tottering towards the church on high heels. Both were attractive and, he guessed, in their late thirties. One had dark hair, the other blonde, and both had the posture of trained dancers. He went to meet them.

'Hello, ladies, I'm Inspector Trevor Joseph.'

KATHERINE JOHN

'We know who you are. It's all over the village.' The blonde bundled the flowers she was carrying into one arm, and shook the hand Trevor offered her. 'I'm Judy Oliver, the vicar's wife.'

'And I'm Angela George.'

'Any relation to Stephen George?' Trevor recalled the name of the officer who had investigated Anna Harris's murder.

'I was. I'm his ex-wife.'

'I'm sorry,' Trevor said.

'I'm not, Inspector Joseph; ten years of being married to a police officer were ten too many. Are you married?' she enquired bluntly.

'Yes.'

'Give your wife my sympathy. Checking the crime scene?'

'Going over the ground covered in the photographs. Both of you ladies knew Anna Harris, didn't you?'

'Everyone knows everyone in Llan, but yes, we knew her and knew her well. We were all in the local amateur dramatic group,' Angela George replied.

'Anna was a lovely girl. Pretty, talented, friendly and thoroughly nice,' Judy Oliver added mechanically as if she were repeating a well-learned lesson. 'Which is rare in someone with her ability. So many would-be actresses think only of themselves.'

'She was just starting out, wasn't she?' Trevor opened the church door for them.

'She'd had a fair bit of experience, nothing big, but we all knew she was going to make it. My husband and I were both in show business, Inspector Joseph.'

'I recognized him.'

'I trained as an actress and dancer, but I was in one of the first girl bands, Boudicca's Babes.'

'I remember them,' Trevor lied.

'And I never made it out of a panto chorus. Would you like to see Anna Harris's memorial?' Angela George kicked a wedge beneath the inner door.

'She's buried inside the church?' Trevor was surprised.

'Everyone in the village felt it was fitting. It was the only thing we could do for her. We organized a collection for a memorial and commissioned a sculptress.' Angela dropped her flowers onto a table and walked down the aisle. To the left of the altar was a raised plinth that held an exquisite marble angel.

Angela gently stroked the cheek. 'The face is Anna's. The sculptress knew her and, of course, Anna's parents had hundreds of photographs.'

Trevor read the inscription.

ANNA LOUISE HARRIS
CRUELLY TAKEN
IN HER EIGHTEENTH YEAR
'THE DAYS OF OUR YOUTH
ARE THE DAYS OF OUR GLORY'

'Byron, Anna's favourite poet, it's taken from...'

'Stanzas written in the road between Florence and Pisa,' Trevor interrupted.

'Wonders will never cease,' Angela muttered. 'I never thought I'd see the day when I'd meet a police officer who reads poetry.'

'Some of us do, Mrs George.' Like Angela, Trevor stroked the angel. Caught up in gathering evidence and interviewing witnesses, it was easy to lose sight of a victim in a murder case. He recalled the beautiful, vibrant girl in the photograph he had shown Peter. He looked down at the angel.

He was disturbed by the thought that Anna's corpse was lying beneath it. He owed it to her, her family and everything she might have been, to find out exactly who had planted David Morgan's axe in her skull.

CHAPTER SIX

TREVOR LEFT THE CHURCHYARD and crossed the road to Church Row. The dozen cottages were detached, thick-walled, each set in its own large garden. They had been built in an age when landowners gave their tenant farm labourers enough land to grow their own food. The Morgans' cottage was the first in the row. Trevor walked up the path and knocked at a wooden door badly in need of a coat of paint. He stepped back and saw that it wasn't only the door that needed painting. The window frames were down to the bare wood in places and half of one of the downstairs frames was boarded up.

The garden had been well planted. Among the weeds he saw mature rose bushes in need of pruning, clumps of lavender, carnations and peonies. It had obviously once been well tended, but like the churchyard it had been neglected. David Morgan's services as gardener and handyman must have been missed by his mother.

When Trevor raised his hand to knock on the door a second time, it was opened. Not by the elderly woman he had expected but a uniformed police sergeant.

'Inspector Joseph,' he introduced himself. 'Is David Morgan at home?'

'Yes, sir. I'm Sergeant Thomas – Mike, with the local force. We're more informal in the country.' He held the door open and Trevor walked directly into a sitting room.

David and his mother were sitting side by side on a flower-patterned sofa. The wallpaper, curtains and upholstery were faded but spotlessly clean, and there were fresh flowers in a vase. The windows were small but they looked out over the back and side as well as the front garden. Given how small they were, the room was surprisingly light.

David jumped up when Trevor entered. But his mother continued to sit, slumped on the sofa, clutching a handkerchief.

'Hello, Mrs Morgan. David, I'm Inspector Trevor Joseph, and I'm here to re-examine the evidence in the murder of Anna Harris.'

'See, Mam, I told you,' David said proudly. 'Mr Smith said the police would send a new officer to prove I didn't kill Anna. He said...'

'David,' Mike broke in. 'I think your mam would like a cup of tea.'

'I'll make one for all of us, shall I, Sergeant

Thomas?' David was as eager to please as a puppy in search of a tit-bit.

'That would be nice, David, thank you.' Mike waited until David was out of the room before handing Trevor a plastic evidence bag containing a sheet of paper. Scrawled in red crayon in childish capital letters were the words, KILLER GET OUT OR BE KILLED. YOU'RE NOT WANTED HERE.

'Has David seen it?' Trevor handed it back to Mike.

'Yes. Not surprisingly it upset him. It was tied around one of these.' Mike held up a second evidence bag containing four large stones.

Trevor took them and examined them through the plastic.

'You can pick up ones like them in any field around here but I thought it as well to ask forensics to check them out.'

'You might strike lucky with DNA.' Trevor handed them back. 'Mrs Morgan, I am sorry. After everything you have been through you shouldn't have to put up with this.'

'I didn't expect people to welcome David back with open arms.' Her voice trembled and she mopped tears from her eyes. 'But after the judge freed him I thought they'd at least let us live in peace. David's suffered so much. He didn't kill Anna.'

David carried in a tray. 'That's why Mr Joseph is here, Mam,' he said cheerfully, 'to prove to everyone in Llan that I didn't.'

'Inspector Joseph, David,' Mike corrected.

'Mr will do.' Trevor looked at Mrs Morgan. 'Is there anyone you can go and stay with for the next few days, Mrs Morgan?'

'I just told Sergeant Thomas. No one's going to drive me out of my own home. They can do what they like. Throw stones at us, break our windows, burn the roof over our heads...'

'There's no need to get upset, Mrs Morgan,' Mike interrupted. 'I told you, I'll have a uniformed officer stationed here, day and night, for the next few days.'

'You have that much manpower?' Trevor was amazed.

'Mrs Morgan's sofa looks comfortable, either I or one of my officers will sleep on it until this is over.'

'Policing in rural Wales is certainly different to what I'm used to, Sergeant Thomas.'

'The case you're working on was the biggest we had in over a century.'

David handed round cups of tea and held

the milk jug and sugar bowl for them to help themselves.

'Please sit down,' Mrs Morgan invited the officers. 'David, there are chocolate biscuits in the cupboard.'

'Not for me, thank you, David.' Mike sat on one of the easy chairs, leaving the one nearest the sofa for Trevor.

'Or me, thank you. I've just eaten one of Mrs James's excellent steaks.' Trevor smiled at David, hoping to put him at his ease. He waited until David had sat next to his mother before speaking to him again.

'I'm here to talk to you about Anna Harris, David.'

'I liked Anna...' David began.

'Anna and David played together when they were children. He was twelve when she was born. He idolised her. Worshipped the ground she walked on. He wouldn't have hurt a hair on her head. He's big but he's always been gentle. They used to call him the gentle giant in special school...'

'I'd like to hear what David has to say, in his own words, Mrs Morgan,' Trevor interrupted softly.

'David's not like other boys, Inspector Joseph.'

'The Inspector knows that, Mrs Morgan.' Mike rose to his feet. 'You said earlier that you needed a few groceries. Why don't I drive you to the superstore?'

'That's ten miles away.'

'Twelve minutes there and twelve back in my car, Mrs Morgan,' Mike smiled. 'And half an hour for shopping. We'll be back within the hour. Inspector Joseph will stay with David until then.'

'I will,' Trevor assured the elderly woman.

'We do need a few things,' she admitted. 'And I don't want to go to Morris's.' She clenched her fists tightly. 'He might refuse to serve me like Tom the baker.'

'Try not to think about it, Mrs Morgan. Get your hat, coat and handbag and we'll be off.' Mike nodded to Trevor, 'See you later, Inspector.'

'I'd appreciate a chat about the locals' view on the case, Sergeant.'

'You're staying in the pub?'

'I am.'

'I'll get one of my constables to cover here for an hour this evening and call in.'

Trevor sat chatting to David about dogs until Mike left with Mrs Morgan. Sammy, the Jack

62

Russell puppy David had been training ten years before was now an old dog. He hadn't moved from his basket the whole time Trevor had been in the room.

'Will you get a new dog, David?' Trevor set his empty tea cup on the tray.

'No point, Mr Joseph.'

'Why's that, David?'

'Can't go out. People don't want to see me.'

'Have you been outside?' Trevor asked.

'Tried when I came home. Went into the garden to sort it. People stood outside the wall and stared at me. Then the children from the council estate came and threw stones. No one stopped them. It upset my mam.' David's bottom lip trembled. 'The garden needs a good going over, so does the churchyard. Mr Tony's been here twice. But he thinks I killed Anna.'

'How do you know, David?'

'Because he keeps saying I've paid for what I've done. He told me and my Mam to hold hands with him and pray. I told him I didn't want to. That I wanted to go out and tidy the churchyard. The stones are all dirty, the grass needs cutting and it needs weeding. He said I can't have my old job back. I told him I'd work for nothing but he said it wasn't up to him but the Church Council.' As David spoke faster his voice rose higher. 'No one in Llan has listened to the judge or Mr Smith. Everyone here still thinks I killed Anna...'

'Tell me about Anna, David,' Trevor interrupted. He found it odd that David grew calmer at the mention of her name.

'Like Mam said, I liked her when she was a little girl. I liked her when she was older too. She was always nice and kind to me. She never made fun of me like some of the other children. We used to play together when she was little, Monopoly, Snakes and Ladders and Ludo. Or cards. Mam likes a game of cards and when Mr and Mrs Harris went away to buy antiques Mam would look after Anna. She slept in the back bedroom and had all her meals with us. But then that was when she was little. I've got a photograph of me and her together. Do you want to see it?'

'Yes, I'd like to.'

'It's upstairs in my bedroom. Mr Smith sent on all my things from prison, but I've tidied them away.'

Trevor followed David into a small hall and up a narrow staircase. David's bedroom was at the side of the house. If Trevor had been asked to guess the age of the occupant he would have put it as early teens. The duvet and matching pillowcase on the single bed were patterned with tigers. The bookshelves filled with comic books, assembled Air Fix kits and framed photographs.

'This is my mam and dad on their wedding day.' David handed Trevor a picture of a couple standing outside a church. The groom's flared trousers dated it as the seventies, but Trevor couldn't help feeling the bride's dress would have been considered old-fashioned, even then.

'What happened to your father, David?'

'He was driving a tractor that fell over on top of him. They took him to hospital but Mam said they couldn't do anything to help him. He died a week later.'

'How old were you?'

'I was a baby. That's why I can't remember him. This is me and Anna Harris. Mam took it on my sixteenth birthday.'

David was holding hands with a small girl with blonde pigtails and Trevor worked out that Anna would have been about four or five years old when it was taken. She was smiling up at David, innocent, trusting. Could David really have killed her fourteen years later?

'It's a nice picture.'

'This is me and Mr Tony the year St David's won an award for being the best kept church in Mid Wales. I'm holding the big cup we won. Mr Tony gave me a small one. Mam keeps it in the cupboard in the parlour.'

Trevor looked David in the eye. 'I know you've told lots of people what happened the day before Anna was killed and the morning you found her. But could you go over it once more with me?'

'Yes, Mr Joseph. Mr Smith...'

'Who's Mr Smith, David?'

'My – my – ' David struggled to get the word out, '– my counsel. He's my friend. He knows I'm innocent and he said I should help the new police officers all I could because you'll prove to everyone that I didn't kill Anna.'

'I promise you, David, I'll do everything I can to find out the truth.'

'I'll make us another nice cup of tea, Mr Joseph and we'll sit in the living room.' He grinned childishly. 'I'll get some of those chocolate biscuits as well.'

He walked down the stairs leaving Trevor to follow. Trevor glanced at the other photographs on the shelf. There was one of David's mother, looking older than her seventy years, her parchment-thin skin stretched over her cheekbones. He recalled her shaking hand, and tremulous voice.

He knew David Morgan must have suffered in prison. He'd seen the regime the warders imposed and the brutality of the inmates firsthand. A man as simple-minded as David would have found it difficult to adjust. He'd be an easy target for cooped-up, frustrated men, and he didn't doubt that David had been bullied. But he could only guess what the last ten years had been like for his mother, stubbornly living on in Llan. Ostracized by most of her neighbours and the local shopkeepers who believed David guilty of the most heinous of crimes.

'Tea's ready, Mr Joseph.'

'Coming, David.' Trevor closed the door on the bedroom and walked down the stairs.

CHAPTER SEVEN

'IT'S LIKE I SAID, Mr Joseph, I didn't look at the girl lying on the ground that morning. Not after I saw she had no clothes on. Mam told me to never look at a naked girl. I didn't know it was Anna Harris until the policeman told me when he locked me away.'

Trevor closed his notebook and pushed his pencil into his pocket. David Morgan must have been asked to tell the story of how he had found Anna Harris's body hundreds of times in the last ten years. Both before and after his trial and conviction. From the files, he knew that David had never changed a single detail. In his experience that meant one of two things. Either David had a brilliant memory and was adept at recalling his lies, or he was telling the truth.

'The earring you found on the path, David. Did you know it was Anna's?'

'No, Mr Joseph. But I knew it was gold. It was dirty. I tried to clean it but I was afraid of scratching it with my nails. I know gold is worth a lot of money.'

'Let's go back to the night before you found Anna in the churchyard. When you were looking for Sammy, did you see anyone?'

'Lots of people. They said they saw me too, in court. Mrs George and Mrs Oliver came out of the Angel Inn and heard me calling Sammy. They'd been to the drama society with all the other ladies. They put on plays in the village. I used to like going to them with my mam. At Christmas they put on pantos. The last one I saw was *Snow White*. It was lovely, Anna Harris was Snow White and... '

'Who else did you see that night, David?' Trevor steered the conversation back on course.

'Mr Tony. He was always going back and forth between the vicarage and the church. There was a choir practice that evening. Mam and me listened to the boys sing when we were having our tea. That was before Mam went to bed with one of her headaches. Mr Morris was outside his shop when I was looking up the road. He was putting rubbish out for the bin men. When I couldn't find Sammy in the High Street or the churchyard I went down the lane to look for him. Mrs Griffiths and Mrs Powell who live in the bottom cottages were gossiping – no – Mam says it's bad to say gossiping. They were talking to each other over the wall.'

69

'It sounds like the whole village was out that evening.'

'In summer if it was hot, it used to be like that. Sometimes until long after it was dark.'

'Did you see Anna?'

'I saw her leave the community centre with the others and go into the Angel Inn. That was before Sammy ran off. We were in the fields. Mr Jones said I could walk Sammy there when there were no animals in them.'

'Did you see Anna afterwards?' Trevor pressed.

'Not until the morning when I didn't know it was her.' David screwed his eyes shut. He had been happy to talk about Anna when she'd been a child but he hadn't said much about her as a young woman. Trevor didn't think that a young woman about to leave home would have much in common with a mentally retarded man, even if they had been playmates when they were younger. A sudden thought occurred to him.

'Did you know that Anna was leaving the village, David?'

David nodded vigorously. 'She told me.'

'How did that make you feel?'

'Sad. But her Mam and Dad were staying, so I thought I'd still be able to do jobs for them.

Anna promised she'd send me postcards. I collect them. I have a book.' He went to a cupboard, opened it and pulled out an album. 'They're from all over the world,' he said proudly. 'Everyone who went on holiday from Llan used to send me and my mam one. There are lots there from Anna.'

Trevor opened the book.

'I put them in as I had them. They're all jumbled but it's easy to spot Anna's. Her mam and dad used to go to the same place every year. In Spain.'

Trevor heard a car pull up outside. He left the sofa and looked above the board that covered the lowered part of the window. He was relieved to see Mike Thomas helping Mrs Morgan out of the passenger seat. If he was going to discover any new evidence, one thing was certain. He wasn't going to find it in the Morgan house.

Peter Collins carried a tray of coffee and biscuits up the stairs of the pub into the makeshift incident room.

'Glad to see you domesticated at last, Collins.' Trevor glanced up from the notes he was making.

'If I hadn't gone down to get it, no one else

would have.' Peter glared at Sarah who was working on the computer.

'Mine's without sugar and a splash of milk.' Sarah hit another button.

'Brainstorming time.' Trevor turned his chair so it faced the other two. 'Caught up with the case, Peter?'

'What I haven't had time to read, Sarah's filled me in on.'

'Good.' Trevor took the coffee Peter handed him. 'Sarah, what do you think we need to do first?'

'Interview Anna Harris's mother, sir.'

'Why?'

'Two things. First, Anna's watch. It has to be significant because of the injuries to her wrist beneath it. But I don't understand why or how they were made.'

'That makes two of us.'

'Three,' Peter added.

'The watch looked unusual. I think it might be worth finding out where she bought it. Or, if it was a present, who gave it to her.'

Peter offered the plate of biscuits to Sarah. 'Anna Harris's mother said in her statement that Anna had several boyfriends. From the post mortem we know she wasn't a virgin and had sex shortly before she was killed. If we are looking for suspects other than David Morgan, a jealous lover would be a classic.'

'You said *two* things, Sarah,' Trevor reminded her.

'Her missing underclothes.'

'Which could be burned or buried in a landfill site. Please don't suggest we carry out a fingertip search for them after ten years,' Peter groaned.

'Suppose she wasn't wearing any? Some girls don't in summer, especially if they're hoping to strike lucky.'

'You're saying she might not have worn underclothes because she intended to have sex that night,' Trevor said carefully.

'Yes.'

'Why don't I ever meet girls who do that?' Peter complained.

'I'll have a word with your girlfriend.'

'Don't you dare, Joseph.'

'Anything else we should ask Anna's mother?' Trevor looked from Peter to Sarah.

'It might be worth making a list of all her boyfriends,' Sarah ventured.

'I agree. Peter, any theories, aside from the jealous lover?'

'We could ask if Anna had enemies. Someone who was jealous of her success. And her father was a wealthy antique dealer. Someone could have had a grudge against him for buying from them too low and selling on to someone else too high.'

'Enough of a grudge to put an axe in his daughter's head?' Trevor picked up his pen.

'Forget I said it,' Peter said, 'I was thinking out loud.'

'I can't see any woman in the village killing Anna so they could take over her role in *The King and I*,' Sarah said.

'Was that show ever performed?' Trevor asked.

'No, and the dramatic society was formally disbanded a month later. There was a notice in the local paper. I asked Mrs James if it ever started up again and she said no one had the heart to even try.' Sarah bit into her biscuit.

"Had the heart." Trevor tried to recall where he had heard that phrase. Then he remembered the vicar had used a similar phrase when he had been talking about keeping the churchyard tidy. 'It seems to me that some of the locals think the heart was torn out of this village when Anna Harris was murdered,' he added, thoughtfully.

Peter opened his notebook. 'So when are you going to see Anna's mother?'

'I'm not.' Trevor turned to Sarah, 'you are.'

'Me?' She looked up in surprise.

'I'm sure Mrs Harris would prefer to be interviewed by a woman. Can you imagine what her reaction might be if Peter or I asked if Anna was wearing underclothes when she was killed?'

'Thank you for having confidence in me, sir. I won't let you down.'

'I know you won't. If you want him to, Peter can accompany you. But it's your call, Sarah. The interview is your responsibility. Set it up as quickly as you can. Today if possible.'

'Yes, sir.'

Trevor scanned his notebook. 'Hopefully Patrick will have some results for us soon from the samples Professor Robbins took. Which leaves the local police. Sergeant Thomas, who replaced Sergeant George when he retired, is coming here this evening to talk to us. In the meantime I'll visit Sergeant, now Mr, George.'

'Do you want me to make an appointment for you, sir?' Sarah asked.

'No thanks, Sarah. I have his address. I'll take a stroll through the village and call in on him. That way I might even get to talk to one or two of the friendly locals.'

'Friendly – some hope,' Peter said sourly.

'Sarah, do we have David Morgan's arrest photographs?'

'Yes, sir. In this file.' She handed it to him. He opened it and looked at the picture.

Peter glanced over his shoulder. 'He looks terrified.'

'Probably because he was. There are no scratches on his face.'

'Is that significant?' Sarah asked.

Trevor closed the file. 'I don't know – yet.'

'You going out as well, Inspector Joseph?' Rita James asked Trevor when he ran down the stairs ten minutes after Sarah and Peter had left the pub.

'Yes, Mrs James.'

'Found out anything yet?' she fished.

'Give us a chance, Mrs James, we haven't been here a day yet,' Trevor pleaded.

'You can have all the chances you want, Inspector. You won't find anything different from what Sergeant George found ten years ago.'

'So everyone keeps telling me, Mrs James. But I wouldn't be doing my job if I didn't try.'

'Anna was such a nice girl. I can't get the last night she was here out of my mind.'

'Why's that?'

'She was so happy. Pleased as punch because she'd got into Drama College and was starring in the local musical. I remember standing by the kitchen window putting glasses into the sink and watching her cross the road after she left here. She was as pretty as a picture and looked as though she didn't have a care in the world. She stopped by the church notice board, took out her hanky and polished the corner of the glass. There must have been a spot of dirt there but that was the kind of girl she was. Do anything for anyone. And she did like the village to look nice. When she was little she used to spend hours in the churchyard with Dai Helpful, picking flowers for the graves that didn't have any. Who would have thought that a few years later Dai would axe her to death and we'd be putting flowers on her grave?'

Trevor couldn't wait to get into the fresh air. He ended the conversation and walked briskly down the street, past the shops. They all had customers and every one of them stared at him. A couple of women even pointed, but he pretended not to see them. He looked straight ahead and kept walking. Retired police sergeant Stephen George lived in the last cottage on the left-hand side of the road through the village.

The "Churchyard Murder" had been Stephen George's last case. The sergeant had taken early retirement at the age of forty, three months after David Morgan's conviction. None of the files had any details as to why Stephen George had left the force so early. Trevor was looking forward to finding out.

CHAPTER EIGHT

TO TREVOR'S SURPRISE, STEPHEN George lived on a working farm, complete with yard and livestock. Stephen was unloading bales of hay from the back of a trailer and carrying them into the barn when Trevor appeared. He dropped a bale and walked to the gate to meet him.

'I can guess who you are.'

Trevor held out his hand. 'Inspector Trevor Joseph.'

'I suppose you want to come inside the house to talk?' Stephen said ungraciously.

'It's a fine day, we can talk out here.'

'You *do* want to talk?'

'Yes.'

'Now?'

'If it's convenient,' Trevor didn't want to appear too pushy.

'I'm about due for a break. And you never know who'll walk past. So you may as well come inside.'

'Thank you.' Trevor opened the gate and stepped warily into the yard. A goat was tethered in the corner but two kids were running free. Flocks of chickens and geese were pecking in the dirt in front of the barn and ducks were swimming on a pond just beyond a side gate. There were pigs in the nearest field and cows in one behind it. 'Is this your farm?'

'Smallholding more than farm. It was my father's. When he had a stroke, I left the force to take over from him. He passed away eight years ago.'

'Nice place.' Trevor meant it. He recognized well-tended stock and an efficiently run farmyard. He'd enjoyed growing up on his parents' farm in Cornwall, but it had been a relief when his younger brother had offered to take over when their father had died. Farming was in his blood but it had never been his ambition.

'The land's good and I get by. It's also why I left the force early.' He eyed Trevor. 'Don't tell me you weren't curious?'

'It's always good to know how a fellow officer managed to get out before time.'

'The next thing you'll be telling me is that you're only doing your job.'

'I am.' Trevor stepped sideways to avoid two cocks who were sizing one another up. 'And, in case you're interested, I didn't ask for this one.'

Stephen George gave a grim smile. 'Knowing the force, I didn't think you did.'

'I would appreciate some background to the David Morgan case.'

'You have the files.'

'In my experience the files only ever give half the story. There's always something left out of official paperwork.'

'Want a beer? It's homebrew, but I can't be bothered to make tea during the day.'

'I'm on duty.'

Stephen kicked his boots off on a stone step. 'You're not one of those straight-laced teetotal coppers, are you?'

'No.' Trevor smiled.

'We'll sit here, in the lean-to.'

Some people might have called the glassed-in area that separated the farmhouse kitchen from the yard a conservatory. "Lean-to" suited it better. It was wooden framed and most of the glass panels were cracked. It was also overflowing with the paraphernalia Trevor associated with farming. Feed invoices, bits of string and strong paper bags, bowls, buckets and shelves full of dusty packets of animal wormers, vitamins and patent medicines.

Stephen lifted a cat from one wickerwork chair and pushed a dog off another. He handed

Trevor a glass and opened a flagon.

'We got the right man. That judge must have been senile to let Dai Helpful out.'

'So everyone in the village keeps telling me.' Trevor sat in the chair the cat had occupied. It promptly jumped on to his lap and curled up contently. He stroked it and it purred, reminding him of home and childhood. 'I met your wife.'

'Ex-wife.' Stephen filled Trevor's glass, then his own. 'This,' he waved his hand in the direction of the yard, 'was to be a fresh start for us. You married?'

'Yes.'

'Then you know how hard it is to make time for your family when the force expects you to cover 24/7. And we're stretched thinner in the sticks than you are in the towns. I hardly ever saw Angela and the kids. My father had the stroke and she gave me an ultimatum, the force or her and the kids. I took her and the kids and this place. My father needed twenty-four-hour care, and had to go into a nursing home. We moved in here. Then Angela and I discovered that after ten years of living separate lives we had nothing in common. Shortly afterwards she moved to her mother's. Then she took up with the geography teacher from the comprehensive. They're getting married on the first of August.'

'That must be tough.' Trevor was suddenly very grateful for his own domestic happiness. It had come as an unlooked-for and astonishing surprise after years spent wondering if he'd ever find a woman who would put up with him – and his job.

'At least she lives close enough for me to see the kids every day. They still come round after school although they'll be off to college soon.'

Trevor sipped the beer. It was warm and tasted foul but he didn't complain. He took his notebook from his pocket. 'Anna Harris's mother made a statement saying Anna had boyfriends. Did you interview any of them?'

'Three or four from the sixth form college.'

Trevor sensed that Stephen George was being guarded. 'She'd had sex the night she died.'

'I read the pathologist's report. She was a healthy attractive eighteen-year-old girl. What did you expect? A nun?'

'Did you pick up on anyone she shouldn't have been having an affair with?'

'Like?' Stephen challenged.

'An older man, possibly married.'

Stephen's face darkened. 'Who have you been talking to?'

'As many people in the village as I can.'

'And they're out to blacken Anna Harris's name when she can't defend herself. That's bloody rich. She was a sweet, kind girl.'

The ferocity of Stephen George's outburst shocked Trevor. 'You loved her?' he asked bluntly.

'I loved her, Tyrone James loved her, Bob Evans loved her. Christ, even the vicar loved her. There wasn't a man in the village who didn't love her. But that doesn't mean we slept with her. You've seen her photographs. She was beautiful. But what the photographs can't show is her personality. One look from her could make you feel good about yourself. A smile and you'd be lost forever. She was Marilyn Monroe and Pollyanna rolled into one.'

'Were you her lover?' Trevor asked bluntly.

'I wish,' Stephen said warmly. 'And you'll probably get the same reply to that question from every man within a fifty-mile radius of Llan.' He set his glass on the flagstone floor.

'You have my word, this is off the record.'

'Off the record?' Stephen George repeated. 'On the record we got the man who murdered her, Dai Helpful. I only wish that the powers that be had the sense to keep him locked up.'

'She'd had sex that night. Someone has to know the identity of her lover.'

'Dai Helpful raped her.'

'The semen samples and pubic hair found on her body were never sent for analysis.'

'We had a strong case. We didn't need further evidence.'

Trevor almost said, "You do things very differently here", but thought better of it. Stephen George was spoiling for a fight, without being pushed.

'What did the women in the village think of Anna?'

'They all adored her.'

'Anna hadn't confided the identity of her lover to any of them?'

'*If* she had a lover other than any of the young boys she went out with, she didn't tell anyone that I heard. Anna was busy studying. She lived for the moment and her ambition to be an actress. I used to see her sometimes being driven home from parties in various boys' cars. There are a lot of wealthy people around here, and not just the landowners. The sort of people who give their sons a top of the range sports car and a Rolex for their eighteenth birthday. Anna was on everyone's party list. She was a popular girl.'

'So I gather.' Trevor abandoned his glass of beer on the floor.

'To go back to your earlier question, Anna was the sort of girl women loved as much as men. I don't mean she was a lesbian. She was in the Angel that night with the women from the Dramatic Society. They'd had a girls only night to rehearse the dances and that should tell you something about her. She had a knack of turning everyone, no matter who or what they were, into a friend. In my opinion that's what killed her. She never treated Dai Helpful any differently from anyone else. He put more store by her friendship than he should have. It's my guess that he saw her with someone in the churchyard that night, spied on them, waited until her lover left and then axed her to death.'

'So you admit she was with her lover in the churchyard that night?'

'I admit nothing. I couldn't prove it but I suspected there might have been someone with her before Dai Helpful turned up. If there was, I never found out who he was.'

'Did you even try?'

'It didn't seem relevant at the time. Not

with Dai Helpful's fingerprints on the axe and Anna's blood on his face. Now, if you'll excuse me, Inspector. I have work to do.'

Trevor walked down the High Street wondering whether to return to Stephen George's farm and ask him outright if he'd had an affair with Anna Harris. Then he saw the barmaid from the Angel, Lily Jenkins, leave the General Store with a box of fruit and vegetables. He ran and caught up with her.

'If you're going to the pub, could I carry that for you?' he offered.

'It's not that heavy, Inspector,' she said shyly.

'It's not that light, either, Lily.' He took it from her. 'What you said today in the bar about Dai Helpful, did you mean it?'

'That he might not have killed Anna Harris? Yes, I meant it, Inspector.'

'Any reason?'

'The judge wouldn't have set Dai Helpful free if he didn't think there was a chance that he hadn't killed Anna.'

'No, he wouldn't have.' Trevor was disappointed that she hadn't come up with something more concrete. 'Do you remember Anna being murdered?'

'I'll never forget it, Inspector.'

'But you were only ten at the time.'

'My sister, Poppy, was the same age as Anna. They used to go everywhere together. Poppy's a teacher now. She lives in London.'

'Did she think that Dai Helpful killed Anna?' Trevor persisted.

'The police said he did. None of us questioned it at the time.'

He recalled what Stephen said about everyone in the village loving Anna. 'You liked Anna?'

'Everyone liked Anna, she was so full of life. But when it came to men...' she fell silent.

'What about Anna and men?' he prompted.

Lily looked over her shoulder to make sure no one was close enough to hear what she was about to say. 'Anna had lots of them. Any one she wanted. She even took Poppy's boyfriend from her. My sister was furious. I was there when they quarrelled about it in our house. Anna refused to take Poppy seriously, she laughed. Then she said, "It's all right, Poppy, I only borrowed him. You can have him back." Of course my sister wouldn't have him back. They were going to get engaged but they never did after that. Poppy still isn't married.'

'So Anna had lots of boyfriends?'

'Dozens, Inspector Joseph. She used to meet one of them in the churchyard. That's why Poppy and I weren't surprised that she'd been found there.'

'How do you know she used to meet someone in the churchyard?'

'Because she told us when we saw her rubbing the marks off the church notice board.'

'What marks?' Trevor recalled what Rita James had said.

She stopped by the church notice board, took out her hanky and polished the corner of the glass. There must have been a spot of dirt there but that was the kind of girl she was. Do anything for anyone. And she did like the village to look nice.

'Anna had one special boyfriend. She wouldn't tell us who he was, only that he was rich and knew everything there was to know about sex. She said the boys in the sixth form college were children compared to him. And when he was free to see her, he used to write the time in a corner of the board with a soft eye- liner pencil she'd given him. If she could make it, she used to rub off the mark and then he'd know she'd be there. You had to look really close to see the numbers. She said he was the only man she could ever love. But not enough to give up her place at Drama School.'

'And you never told Sergeant George any of this at the time?'

'He never asked, Inspector. Besides, everyone thought Dai Helpful killed Anna.'

CHAPTER NINE

TREVOR WAS WATCHING THE video of Anna's funeral in the incident room when Peter and Sarah returned from visiting Anna's mother. He glanced at his watch.

'I was just about to go down to order dinner.'

'Can you wait?' Sarah's eyes were shining.

'He can wait if it's going to get him back to his lady love sooner than he thinks.' Peter set a box on the table.

Sarah saw Trevor looking at it. 'The watch, sir. Anna's mother gave it to us.'

'It was in a box of Anna's effects the police handed back to her family.' Peter held up a bag. 'Sarah also persuaded her to part with the dress. It's still in the police evidence bag.'

'Good work, Sarah.' Trevor looked at the screen. Judy Oliver was standing next to Anna's coffin, reciting a poem. She was dressed formally but there was something odd about her shoes. He made a note to think about it later, before switching off the TV.

'I talked to Anna's mother by myself, sir, as you suggested.' Sarah took her own notebook from her handbag. She flipped it open. 'She said that as far as she could make out none of Anna's underclothes were missing. And she told Sergeant George that.'

'Which is why the local police never issued a description of them,' Collins said. 'They didn't know what they were looking for.'

'Anna's mother admitted that Anna rarely wore underclothes in summer in the evening. She also said she had never seen the watch before the police showed it to her.' Sarah turned over the page. 'She was certain no one in the family had given it to Anna. She'd celebrated her eighteenth birthday two months before she was killed, but her mother can't recall seeing a watch like it among the presents. She couldn't say for definite that it wasn't Anna's because her daughter had a lot of jewellery. She said,' Sarah referred to her notes, '"Boys were always giving Anna jewellery. She put the boxes in the top drawer of her dressing table."'

'Didn't she know the watch was valuable?' Trevor asked.

'The only value Mrs Harris puts on Anna's possessions is sentimental, sir. It was painful to listen to her talking about her daughter – and her husband. As she said, one day she was running a successful antiques business with a loving husband, beautiful daughter and comfortable home. The next she was burying her daughter and days later her husband. He took an overdose of sleeping pills after Anna's funeral. She couldn't bear to return to the village, so she sold the business and her home.'

'Then Anna never wore the watch in front of her parents.' Trevor felt that his theory of a married lover had just gained strength.

'When Mrs Harris moved, she boxed up Anna's things. She couldn't bear to throw them away so she put them in her spare bedroom. She took me up there and we went through them together. We found an empty jewellery box with an oval indentation.'

'It fits the watch?'

'It could do, sir. I thought you might want to send the watch to be checked out for DNA so I didn't handle it. I left it in the police evidence bag, as I did with the dress.'

'Excellent, Sarah. You have the makings of a first class detective,' Trevor complimented.

'There's a name on the box. Evan Evans and Jones. It's a local high class jeweller's.'

'Where are they based?' Trevor asked.

93

'Llandeilo.'

'You and Peter can go there first thing tomorrow.' Trevor stopped talking when he heard a footstep outside. There was a knock at the door.

'Inspector Joseph?'

'Please come in, Mrs James.'

'Mike – Sergeant Thomas – is downstairs. He asked me to let you know. And I was wondering if you're coming down for dinner. The specials are swordfish and boar steaks. We're running out of both fast.'

'We're coming, Mrs James.' Trevor pocketed his notebook.

'I take it we can't trust this local copper further than we can see him,' Peter said.

'I don't know,' Trevor said cautiously. 'He certainly knows the village and the people but he might be protective of his force's history.'

'Is he straight?'

'That's the question everyone wants to ask every copper, Sergeant Collins.' Sarah Merchant, like all the officers in their station, knew just how often Peter Collins "bent" the rules to get results.

'Let's give him the benefit of the doubt and take him at face value,' Trevor said.

'But we don't discuss any of our findings with him?'

'That goes without saying, Collins.'

Mrs James had meant it when she'd told them the kitchen was in danger of running out of specials. The dining room was packed with local people. Trevor saw ex-Sergeant George sitting at a table with the retired farmer Bob Jones. Tony Oliver was with Angela George and another man who Trevor assumed was the geography teacher Angela was about to marry. There was no sign of Judy Oliver. Gareth Morris the newsagent was with Tom the baker and two women Trevor took to be their wives.

Mike Thomas was waiting for them at the bar. Trevor introduced Peter and Sarah.

After they had shaken hands, Mike said, 'I asked Rita to set us up a table in the back bar. There's no one in there and there won't be until the dominoes club arrives at half past nine. One pint and three games are the social highlight of the week for some of the OAPs around here.'

They followed him into a room containing four tables and sixteen chairs. As Mike had said, it was deserted.

'I can't stay long,' Mike warned. 'I've put in my order for boar steak, chips and salad. If you're into unusual starters I recommend the laver bread and oatmeal wrapped in bacon.'

'Seaweed.' Peter made a face.

'It's good, Sergeant Collins.'

'Why don't you and Sarah go and order for us, Peter? I'll have the same as Sergeant Thomas.' Trevor sat down. 'You have someone with the Morgans?'

'Constable Alan Williams, he's experienced but I'm not expecting trouble this evening. There are too many people out and about in the village. If anything happens it will be when everyone's asleep and I'll be there.'

'I hope you have a quiet night,' Trevor said sincerely.

'Were you in the force when Anna Harris was murdered, Sergeant Thomas?' Peter Collins set pints of Guinness in front of himself and Trevor. Sarah followed with mineral water for herself and Mike.

'It was the first case I worked on. I was a rookie of nineteen. I dug out my notebook for that year for you.' He took it from his pocket.

'Can you remember the case?' Trevor moved a beer mat beneath his glass.

'Very well. It shook everyone in the county.

Not that we hadn't had serious crimes in Mid Wales before, but most of them were domestic. Farmers killing their wives and vice versa. I remember being surprised that all the samples the pathologist took weren't sent to the lab. Professor Robbins was meticulous. I watched him do the post-mortem. Part of my training,' he explained.

'We've all been through it.' Peter took a long pull at his pint.

'I asked Sergeant George why he was only sending some of the samples for analysis. He said there was no point in testing everything because it was obvious that David Morgan was guilty. More lab work would only add to the cost of the investigation and eat into our budget which was already stretched.'

'What samples are you thinking of in particular?' Trevor asked.

'The watch that had been strapped on to her wrist after death.'

'You knew about the injuries beneath it?'

'You couldn't miss them once the watch was removed. And there were semen stains on her dress. I thought it might be as well to check them against David's blood type. DNA wasn't in common use – not here anyway, not back then.'

'Anything else?'

'Reading through the notes I made at the time it struck me that I would investigate a similar case – not that I want one thank you very much – differently now. But the force has changed a great deal in the last ten years.'

Lily came in with their meals and Mike waited until she had served them before continuing. 'As I said, I was nineteen when Anna Harris was murdered, Inspector. I didn't move in the same circles she did, but I knew who she was.'

'There's a social pecking order in this backwater?' Collins smothered his boar steak with redcurrant jelly.

Mike laughed. 'The class war is well and truly alive and well in Mid Wales, sergeant. The moneyed *crachach*...'

'The what?' Peter demanded.

'*Crachach* – it's Welsh for elite or toffs – send their children to private or Welsh-medium schools. They don't mix with the kids from the council estates where I come from. The two factions don't drink in the same pubs or even buy in the same shops. But I knew Anna Harris by sight and reputation.'

'What sort of reputation?' Trevor suspected he already knew the answer to his question.

'For sleeping around. But she was choosy. According to one of my friends who worked as a TV extra alongside Anna, she was star-struck and ambitious. Her nickname in the studios in Llandaff was "Brutus" because she'd stab anyone in the back to get ahead. There were rumours she'd have sex with anyone who would introduce her to a producer or director. Some even said she slept her way into Drama College, but I think that was jealousy coming from the ones who didn't get in.'

Trevor was instantly on the alert. 'Any ideas who these "anyone" were?'

'As I said, I didn't know her personally. It could be no more than idle gossip.'

Collins wiped his lips with his napkin. 'More killers have been caught through idle gossip than interrogation, Sergeant Thomas.'

'Excuse me.' Mike Thomas answered a ring on his mobile. He listened for a few seconds, then barked. 'I'll be there. Two minutes.'

'The Morgan house?' Trevor asked.

'Lynch mob. Williams has sent for back-up.'

Trevor was already out of his chair. 'We'll drive you.'

The Morgan house was engulfed by a crowd of angry people. Trevor had expected teenagers, but there were a hundred or more people of all ages, from elderly men and women down to babies in pushchairs who had been brought there by their mothers.

Mike Thomas left the car and held his hands up in an appeal for calm. But the mob carried on shouting, screaming insults and throwing sticks and stones. A uniformed constable was standing in front of the house desperately trying to look as though he wasn't concerned by what was happening. Trevor noticed that all the missiles that were being thrown were landing well clear of him. But two garden gnomes, half buried in weeds, had lost their heads.

Mike Thomas didn't attempt to fight his way through the mob. He simply tapped the shoulders of the people in front of him. They turned, saw him and moved aside. He was soon standing alongside his colleague on the doorstep.

Collins went to follow, but Trevor held him back.

Mike started to speak, quietly in his normal voice. A hush descended.

'You all know who I am. I don't know what you're doing here...'

'Driving out a killer,' a man shouted.

100

'Before he murders our daughters and sisters,' someone else screamed.

'Shut up,' another yelled. 'Let the sergeant speak.'

'David Morgan has served time in prison. A judge has set him free...'

'To kill again,' a woman screeched hysterically.

'Do you think he's likely to do that, Mrs Protheroe, with Constable Williams and me watching him? We'll be here all night I promise you.'

'Then he's under house arrest?'

'David is a free man, he can go wherever he wants to.'

'Then why are you here?'

'To stop you lot ending up in court for grievous bodily harm – or worse. Go home and leave the policing to the professionals. That's a polite request. Otherwise, in one minute I'll be out there with my notebook booking people for public affray.'

'They're here to whitewash Dai Helpful.' Mrs Protheroe pointed at Trevor, Sarah and Peter.

'They're here to reopen the case. Standard procedure when a judge remits a sentence, Mrs Protheroe. Good evening.'

'Bloody bootlickers,' she muttered as she passed Trevor.

'And a good evening to you, too, Madam,' Peter called after her.

Trevor waylaid a young boy. 'Whose idea was it to come here?'

The boy shrugged his shoulders.

'You can do better than that,' Trevor coaxed.

'Someone overheard Mr George, Mr Morris and Reverend Oliver talking in Morris's shop. They said Dai Morgan's going to get millions in compensation for going to prison. He'll be free, rich and laughing and Anna Harris will be left rotting in her grave.'

CHAPTER TEN

'Do you have an eye-liner pencil I can borrow?' Trevor asked Sarah as they were leaving the breakfast table the next morning.

'Any particular colour, sir?'

'I didn't know they came in different colours.'

'Electric blue might be his shade,' Peter suggested.

Sarah rummaged in her handbag and handed Trevor a black pencil.

'Thank you.' Trevor slipped it into his shirt pocket.

'I suppose it's too much to ask what it's for,' Peter said.

'It is. Enjoy yourself at the jeweller's.'

Trevor went upstairs and telephoned Mike Thomas in the Morgan house. After Mike assured him that there had been no more disturbances during the night, he switched on the TV. He was watching the film of Anna's funeral again when the telephone rang. He picked it up.

'Trevor Joseph.'

'And this is your favourite pathologist.'

'Patrick, good to hear from you. Any results?'

'Where do you want me to start?'

'The wrist injury beneath the watch.'

'Robbins took swabs. There were glass, gold and stone fragments mixed in with blood and bone. The blood tested positive for Anna Harris. The gold was nine carat, the slivers of glass thin and polished.'

'Like a watch face?

'Exactly.'

'But the watch was intact.'

'I keep telling you...'

'You deal in facts. The semen and pubic hair?'

'The DNA in the semen was fragmented but what we have matches the hair. Give us a suspect and we can clear or identify him as the man who had sex with Anna Harris the night she was murdered. Your boys are running it through your database. As of ten minutes ago there were no matches. But the database was only started in 2003. If he hasn't committed a crime since then, there won't be a match on file.'

'It's not David Morgan's.'

'No, he gave samples voluntarily and

permission for us to keep them on file. His solicitor hoped they would prove his innocence. They certainly prove he didn't have sex with Anna Harris that night. Ask me about the tissue under the fingernails.'

'You found a DNA profile?'

'Partial. It doesn't match the pubic hair or semen. There were traces of nail varnish mixed in with it. Bright red. It's possible Anna Harris clawed her attacker's hand.'

'I have the watch and the dress she was wearing when she was killed. They're still in police evidence bags. If we need any tests, you'll interpret the findings?'

'Anything I can do, anytime, you know that Trevor.'

'Thanks, Patrick, much appreciated.'

Trevor made a few more notes. Wanting to take another look at the churchyard, he went downstairs.

Rita James came out from behind the bar and waylaid him in the hall. 'Nasty business that, at the Morgans' last night.'

'It was, Mrs James.'

'Mike Thomas and Constable Williams were both there all night.'

'So I understood from Sergeant Thomas this morning.'

'You telephoned him then?'

'First thing.'

'Lily,' Rita James stopped the barmaid as she was leaving the kitchen. 'Get the flowers and chocolates Stephen George brought yesterday and put them on the Olivers' lunch table.'

'Celebration?' Trevor asked.

'Judy Oliver's birthday.'

'And Stephen George sends her flowers?'

'They are brother and sister, Inspector.'

'Of course,' he frowned. 'When I first met Angela George and Judy Oliver they told me they were sisters-in-law.'

'Closer than most sisters despite the divorce. You going out?' she enquired.

'For a while, Mrs James.'

Trevor stood outside the pub and tried to imagine himself inside Anna's mind. He crossed the road and looked at the church notice board. He took the pencil Sarah had given him and made a mark on the glass. It was difficult to see what the mark was. But the pencil dulled the glass and it was easy to see it had been smudged. A clever way of signalling provided no one cleaned it, and that wasn't very likely.

He walked up to the shed and sat on the tomb. Thoughts whirled at breakneck speed through his mind. Patrick had proved from the evidence left on Anna's body that she had met two people after she had left the pub that night. Evidence Stephen George had deliberately withheld. First, the man she had made love with. A man who had no police record, and who might – or might not – have given her the watch. Definitely a man who didn't want to be publicly linked to her. Possibly because he was married.

Then she met her murderer, who could be identified because Anna had scratched him before she died. The proof of his identity had lain beneath her fingernails. Why hadn't Stephen George sent the scrapings for analysis? Had Anna's lover already left her when the murderer struck?

Trevor imagined Anna alone where he was sitting. The murderer creeping up behind her. It would be dark around the tomb even in moonlight. If he had come from behind the yew tree she might have heard him but not seen him until he had struck her. And then it would have been too late. A single blow, Patrick had said. She would have fallen but she took minutes to die, minutes when she reached out –

He recalled the film of Anna's funeral service, leapt off the tomb, ran back into the pub and up the stairs.

'You all right, Inspector?' Mrs James called after him.

'Perfectly, Mrs James.' He closed the door and switched on the TV and DVD player.

'Come on,' he muttered as he flicked through the tracks.

'Have we got news for you, Joseph?' Peter walked in, Sarah close behind him.

'Just a moment.' Trevor found the track he wanted and pressed play.

Judy Oliver was standing in front of the altar, facing Anna's coffin and the congregation. Pale, trembling, her voice rang out clearly. The voice of an actress trained to perform no matter what her personal feelings.

'And thou art dead, as young and fair
As aught of mortal birth;
And form so soft, and charms so rare
Too soon return'd to earth!
Though Earth received them in her bed,
And o'er the spot the crowd may tread
In carelessness and mirth,
There is an eye which could not brook
A moment on that grave to look...'
'Elegy on Thyrza, by Anna's favourite poet,

Lord Byron,' Sarah murmured, touched by Judy Oliver's rendering.

Trevor didn't hear her. He was staring at Judy Oliver's feet. She was wearing brown sandals. They didn't look right with her formal black dress. But it was obvious why she was wearing them. Across the bridge of her right foot was a bandage.

'You'll never guess what we discovered,' Peter said when Trevor switched on the TV.

'There were two watches,' Trevor said.

'How did you know?' Sarah looked at him in admiration.

'Patrick found traces of a second watch in the wound on Anna's wrist. I know who bought them, but is there a record?'

'They were expensive, the buyer paid in cash, but,' Sarah smiled, 'I insisted they went through the files. The owner didn't remember the sale but his father did.'

'And he'll swear in court that Tony Oliver bought them?'

'Won't you give us credit for anything, Joseph?' Peter grumbled.

'Lily told me that Anna had one special boyfriend who was rich and knew everything there was to know about sex. Mike Thomas said there were rumours that Anna would have sex with anyone who would introduce her to a producer or director. There's only one man in the village who has strong connections with show business. But he slipped up when he bought similar, if not identical, watches for his wife and girlfriend.'

'I still don't see...'

'You will. Telephone Mike Thomas. Tell him you're arresting Judy Oliver for the murder of Anna Harris. She may be downstairs having lunch.'

'Where are you going?' Peter asked irritably when Trevor opened the door.

'To arrest the man who covered up the crime and perverted the course of justice.'

Stephen George was sitting in his lean-to, drinking beer. Trevor rapped on the glass. Stephen opened the door. He looked Trevor in the eye and Trevor saw that he knew what was coming. But George made one last, half-hearted attempt at bravado.

'More questions, Inspector Joseph?'

'Just one. Did Tony Oliver help you to cover up your sister's murder of Anna Harris?'

'No.'

'Is that the truth?'

'Yes.' Stephen returned to his chair. 'I knew when Dai Helpful won his appeal it might only be a matter of time. I would have destroyed the samples Professor Robbins took at the post-mortem, if I'd known where they'd been sent. As the years passed, I hoped they'd been thrown out.'

'Did you see Judy kill Anna?'

'No. She telephoned me on her mobile. She was hysterical. I thought she'd caught Tony sleeping with another woman. He was always playing around. Judy said she was in the churchyard. I walked there and found her sitting on a tombstone looking at Anna's body. I don't think she realized she'd killed Anna until she stamped on the watch with her stiletto heel and tore Anna's earrings from her ears. Tony had bought Anna those as well. When Anna didn't move or make a sound, Judy snapped. That's when she telephoned me.'

'Whose idea was it to put Judy's watch on Anna's wrist?'

'Mine. Judy said people had seen Anna wearing the watch in the pub. I sent Judy home to get hers to replace the one she'd broken. I thought the smashed watch an obvious indication that a jealous wife was the killer.

And Judy was known to be jealous. Tony gave up his career when Judy was charged with assaulting one of his mistresses. She couldn't cope with all the girls he worked with. With good reason. He always had at least one, if not more, on the go.'

'And he couldn't resist Anna.'

'I told you the truth when I said we were all in love with Anna. But she was choosy. She wanted to be a star. Tony still knew a lot of people in the business.'

'Only he became careless and Judy found out.'

'She was suspicious of every woman he looked at or talked to. That night she saw Anna wearing an identical watch to one he'd given her. She went home and found the receipt for both of them and a pair of earrings in his desk drawer. She went to the church intending to confront him. She saw him locking up after choir practice but, instead of going home, he went to the back of the shed. She hid behind the yew tree and waited.'

'And saw him with Anna.'

'The axe was in the chopping block behind the tree. Dai had only chopped half a load of logs and hadn't locked it away. I'm not blaming him...'

112

'That's big of you, considering he served ten years in prison for a crime your sister committed. You fitted him up, George.'

'Not intentionally. I tore Anna's dress off her to make it look like a rape that had gone too far. I planned to investigate it and find nothing. Dozens of murders remain unsolved across the country every year. Only Tony phoned me when he found Dai with Anna's body the next morning. It was perfect.'

'Not for Dai Helpful.'

'He'll get compensation.'

'I'll visit you after you've served ten years inside and ask what price you'd put on ten years in prison, George.'

Two days later, Trevor carried his case and a box of files down to his car at seven in the morning. Rita James was in the hall.

'Constable Merchant said you're checking out today, Inspector.'

'After one of your excellent breakfasts, Mrs James. Peter and Sarah will be down shortly.'

'I'm sorry. But who would have thought a woman like Judy Oliver capable of murder? I know she'd been in show business, but she was still a vicar's wife. Here let me.' She opened the door for him. 'Give me your keys and I'll unlock your car.'

Trevor rested the box on his knee, ferreted in his pocket and handed them over. They both glanced at the church. David Morgan was struggling with the lock on the shed door.

'He's a forgiving soul,' Rita murmured.

'Seeing the churchyard in a state upset him.' Trevor locked the box and case in the boot of his car, crossed the road and walked up the path. David had knocked the lock off the shed and was looking inside.

'It's empty, Mr Joseph.'

'I expect the Church Council will soon buy you some new tools.'

'That's what Mam said. Thank you, Mr Joseph. Mr Smith said you'd prove that I didn't kill Anna and you did.'

'I'm only sorry it wasn't sooner, David.'

'I picked these in Mam's garden for Anna.' David pulled a small bunch of roses from his pocket. 'Do you think she'd like them?'

'I do, David – and it's her, not me, you should be thanking. All the evidence we needed was on her body.'

David opened the door of the church, took off his cap and went inside. Trevor watched him walk up to the tomb. He turned back and saw Mrs Morgan standing on the path. She held out her hand. He shook it. Below him Peter and Sarah were loading Sarah's van.

'Goodbye, Mrs Morgan.'

'Goodbye, Inspector Joseph. Thank you and may God bless you.'

He smiled at her. 'I rather think he already has, Mrs Morgan.'

SECRETS

BY LYNNE BARRETT-LEE

Sisters Megan and Ffion have never had secrets, so when Megan goes to flat-sit all she's expecting is a rest and a change.

When a stranger called Jack phones, Megan wonders who he is. Ffion behaves like she's just seen a ghost, and refuses to say any more.

So is Jack a ghost? Ffion's not telling and when she disappears too, the mystery deepens. Megan begins to fear for the future. She's always been the one who has looked after her little sister. Is this going to be the one time she can't?

LYNNE BARRETT-LEE is the author of four novels and also writes as Daisy Jordan for Transworld. She lives with her family in Cardiff, Wales.

ISBN 1905170300
price £2.99